"Original, distinctive, and quirky, there's something legendary about Kate's writing. 'Writing' doesn't fully describe the evocative prose, it sings off the page with the sultriness of a Hollywood starlet and raps with the cool of the Rat Pack. I can't decide if she carries her pen in a holster on her stockinged thigh or in a violin case alongside her Tommy gun."

—*Matt Hilton, author of the international bestseller Joe Hunter thrillers*

"Fair warning—you are about to be enveloped by a whirlwind. A soft whirlwind of words and snappy patter and hoods wide shouldering the front seat of midnight sedans and a ball player on the outs and back ins and gats and tommyguns of the 45 persuasion ratatat-tating and the best cuppa joe in the world and a rock hard chunk of chocolate that ain't candy and Sinatra croonin' and Wind-song all over your mind and some secret and not-so-secret agents...and...and...and if this all sounds confusing, just keep in mind what Nelle Towse Callahan tells ya right out in front: 'Something's up. Something always is.' Remember that and you'll be all right, bub. You will be exactly all right."

—*A.J. (Bill) Hayes, revered crime-noir author of our thriller times, who left us in shadows way too damn soon*

23 September 2017

Janice —
Watch out for those delusions.

THE DAMP FEDORA

They're never all they're cracked up to be... Or are they?

Do Enjoy Noirvella 1 of 8

love,
Kate & Merle

KATE PILARCIK

THE DAMP FEDORA

NOIRVELLA #1
OF A SERIAL OF INTRIGUE

DOWN&OUT
BOOKS

Down & Out Books
3959 Van Dyke Rd, Ste. 265
Lutz, FL 33558
www.DownAndOutBooks.com

Cover design by Jason Smith

ISBN: 1-943402-41-8
ISBN-13: 978-1-943402-41-0

With a fond dedi'kation to Prof,
historian Matthew S. Magda,
who believed writing flowing like water
should be published; then published again

With a respected dedi'kation to Chief,
publisher Eric Campbell,
who is doing so; then doing so again,
flourishing Nelle's noirvella intrigue into serials

Both esteemed gents deserve
the best cup o' joe a rainy night can brew,
and the first one said, "Marry me, will you?"

PROLOGUE
GAL GUMSHOE'S GOT GUMPTION

Hello there. Cop a seat. Sit a spell. They call me Nelle. Nelle Callahan. I'm a private eye with a penchant for winking trouble's way. I can load a Luger or lead on a loser without looking over my shoulder, come the end of a coffee and doughnut day. That's how they come at you. When you least expect it. But you knew that. You're no flimflam or chump. You're jake.

And stories? Every sucker behind the eight ball's got a soppy one. You think they're on the up and up? No way, Buster Brown. Not even when those crumbums hit the pavement and eyeball their bottom dollar, sucking up their last breath with their puss down. Every bird is workin' an angle, I tell ya.

My job? Cut through some slick con's shadow, lift a corner of chintz off the mist, let some truth shine in for the chippies and the chopper squad—you know—menfolk who measure themselves by how big their tommy guns *really* are. Yeah. You get my drift. Everyone's a dreamer. And everyone wants to grill their beef. They amble in to see me when they

1

don't know the diff and wanna get someplace where they're not. Usually in a jiff. You can see 'em comin' like butter and eggs men. You know the type, the rubes and yokels who flash big wads in nifty nightclubs and wonder what hit 'em on a not so nifty night. Usually it was a .45.

1945.

World's got a whole new spin. Me and Jake, who *was* jake—we used to drink out of the same bottle—you know what I mean, we were close, real close. Pitchin' woo. Well, 'til the cheap floozy in glad rags sashayed our big picture. She was no satin doll—I'll tell you that. But I don't wanna get into *issues* right now. Man oh man, was I miffed. I wanted to tell that damn Jake Devlin to dust off, take his gat and git. But there was a flaw to my fine falutin' cogitating there.

Flaws and troubles come at you when you think your good idea is the one hot potato that's gonna bounce you from the bumps on rough stretches. The trouble with watching Jake's trench trudge out our door was...well, he's still my partner. And his uncle, Harvey, heck, he's our landlord. Gee whiz, I really like Uncle Harvey. I think he's swell. It's his nephew janglin' my nerves like bangtails at the Belmont, come post time. I think I need a diversion.

THE DAMP FEDORA

It was raining that night in the City by the Bay. A hard rain. The kind of rain that washes regrets from men's souls and streams chalk lines off city sidewalks. I was in my office, waiting for the phone to ring-a-ding-ding. I had just completed a case which had me peeking from behind the Iron Curtain under cover so deep I'd almost forgotten my own name. But it was worth it. I had stopped a war, broke a Ukrainian heart, and made enough lettuce to put me straight with some old and very unpleasant acquaintances. Now that I'd paid my landlord the rent I owed on my office, I was finally back up to broke, on the nut, and needing some new action—fast.

I heard the crunch of his Florsheims before I saw his silhouette go rugged behind the frosted glass of my office door. He rapped that glass like he meant it.

"It's open," I called out.

He stepped in like the breeze off a good Narragansett sail. Strutted his stuff just as robust.

Blew bravado clean over my desk. "You Callahan?" he barked.

"That's how it reads on the door, Mister," I remarked.

"I'm looking for something. You find *somethings*?" He challenged like a chip with a man on its shoulder. You could cut his bluster with heavy-duty Ace power tools. Yet, timing's timing. I knew my stuff. I let his bluster muster and his jets cool. Hell, I'm no fool.

"That's the business I'm in. What's the searching you're for?"

Only sound was the scratch of his match. To make it darb, he did it smack dab off the side o' my mahogany desk. Nope, flinching wasn't in me, nor was his check if I did. *So, wise guy, that's how it's gonna play.* He took a deep drag on a Pall Mall. I actually had places to go and promises to keep on keeping on, but not the desire right now, to have it known.

Nix on that. Why, I'd bet the George Washington under my steel file cab—yep, my bottom dollar—this bub was going to prove *very* interesting. Time wasn't on my side though to wait out his tease-test. At the split sec the ash got too big for itself, the ruby manicure of my left hand slid a cobalt crystal ashtray his way, while my right hand readied accoutrements to become my write hand. My canary yellow legal pad slid several inches closer. The curious yellow canary in our office cage feathered itself likewise.

"Your name?" I lobbed him an easy one right off the bat.

"Me? I could be any Tom, Dick or Harry...hell, even just your average Joe," he parried. A no-nonsense look leveled away his nonsense. Our eyes locked for just a split. No blink, no flinch. Same bottom GW ruled out "Joe" right away. No profile fit *average* on this bub.

"Howzabout I simply call you *Harry* until all four of you figure who steps forward?"

Imperceptible smile mingled and morphed to perceptible gauntlet. His upper hand? Showboated his display and delay technique with a slow-mo grasp of what was on top of his mind. Then a dramatic doff of his dampened fedora. He positioned it on my desk. Carefully, precisely. Centered it even. His definition of authority. Didn't take long for a soggy spot to mar my mahogany. I hate when someone messes with my mahogany. Matter of pride. Matter of principle. As a matter of fact I deduced this darn rogue's tryin' to get under my skin.

His bushier eyebrow challenged. The one on the left.

I quirked back, double-time. Mine was right.

Statements understated are best understood. "Harry it is," his voice lowered, the timbre of pillow talk. Ticked me off, that talk. Reminded me of my partner—well, *former* mush partner, still stuck-as-a-gumshoe partner—Jake. Since that jingle-brained chippy chirped his nest, things were no longer jake with Jake. Timbre like that's tough to take. Timbre that makes you fall hard once, causes your caution to take root, branch out. Didn't know who was going to get a rise out of what first, but no one was seeing this dame flap under the warmth of any cool breezer.

"Fine. I ever get wild over you, I'm all set with lyrics." Now, to burst the urge of grandstanding his non-expression-expressing all over again, plus encourage his damn damp fedora off the new puddle on my old mahogany, a change of venue was in order. Time to blow.

"Cup o' joe, Harry?"

~ ~ ~

Trenches kept stride. Professional pride, ya know. No tippin' of the mitts goin' on here. We gave each other the old ups-and-downs alongside gutters of silent slosh running up State Street, that gritty dim fate street. *Even shadows know who's boss on a mean street.*

"Tough place. People seem bewildered by the world they behold here." His dour observation edged the cool night air the rough rain had plumb forgot to freshen up.

Redolent of the way the wind's song played my mind, my retort shot back in the same temp as disheartened air...

"Well, Harry, that's what a town without pity will do."

THE WILL'S THE WAY

As we look into our tale of two trenches trudging their tough night, the rain-washed streets are easing some pain-washed minds. So it seems. Well, so it seems. It's not always as it seems, though. But it seems so Here. Now. On this street...on this night. Doesn't it?

~ ~ ~

"Mean streets, Callahan? But aren't today's mean streets the de facto version of yesterday's chivalric forests? We all have to travel them. Immerse ourselves in destructive danger elements to emerge tougher, more resilient...a finer version formed from our former selves. More mindful of what the world's handing out, dealing down. Sometimes the dealing's down and dirty. Sometimes it's dealt aces straight up. We travel them both, the mean streets and those pesky forests which tend to bewilder. All to discover where we're headed ourselves," ruminated the indistinct man under the dampened fedora.

He paused pace without warning. Quick Florsheim skid, like he wanted to take measure of how his words weighed in. *To me, or to himself?* His tall shadow held, dominating liquid light flickering up the mist 'neath a rickety grey lamp post. He pulled his deck. Lit his Lucky. Made me wonder why this sport sported two different brands of cigs. Each with a reach from different pockets. Time would tell. Time always squeals greater truths—like bald tires on pavements of wrong roads turned into.

His solemn scrutiny took in all the perimeters. The parameters too. This was not a street corner of optimum desire. "Uh, it is *Miss* Callahan?"

"Intriguing take there, *Mister* Harry. You're a tough guy with a lotta learnin' under that soggy fedora. And yes. No miss on Miss. Proud of skirting slippery slides down pitfalls of matrimonial slopes. There are collisions that stop your heart and there are long lonesome highway crashes of the bad road variety. But why am I telling *you* this, buster? You're a guy who's obviously been around, meandered his forests and mean streets, and yet seems able to string together words with more than two syllables. There are days that feat is literally remarkable to come across in my line of work. Now, about this finding *something* you're looking for—"

~ ~ ~

The 1944 dark DeSoto with the hulking front grill grin skiddled the middle of the puddle off the curb near the confab of the detective and her new client, a tall talking man—itching, though patiently so, with something to reveal to get to something that he needed. The itchy quiet talker was a rumpled but ruggedly handsome man preferring to be hailed by the nondescript moniker of "Harry" for the time being. No telling yet who this non-Harry really was, nor how close he trenched his storylines. No time to read through any of those wrinkled lines right now. A strong arm indicating bad business extended further menace from the DeSoto's front passenger window. Took a shot in the dark to stage a near miss near Miss Callahan. No mistaking that miss. *Warnings seldom are.*

Nelle stepped into the street. Stooped low. Plucked a slug from a .45 still spinning against the curb as the car spun speedy its getaway. No plates. She'd bet a berry it was a bent car on the lam. Looked like three goons inside. With all the shoulders attached.

"Friends of yours, Callahan?"

"I've made a few along my way, sure. But, howzabout you? Anyone know of all the dick joints on all the rainy streets in the world...you were gonna walk into mine tonight?"

"I was pondering that point myself, Nelle. I *can* call you *Nelle* now, correct? We've just had our first share of lead squirt our way. In certain places, like Bolivia, that's as mutually bonding as riffling a ripe romance. Now, could this fine establishment be our coffee shop?"

"Sure, sure, you got the right to call me Nelle, Mr. Wise Guy. And yessiree. This is it, Hill O' Beans. Best cup o' joe a dark rainy night can brew. You'll see. I know my coffee, I like my coffee. Provides perk and pause to ruminate. You ruminate a helluva lot too, rather than just bumping gums, don't ya, Harry?"

~ ~ ~

Albert DeFonse Magruder heard the tiny silver bell tinkle again above the doorway to where he brewed the best beans this seaside town sipped and savored. Despite the drench of trenches dripping fresh rivulets on tired linoleum under the Hill O' Beans' coat tree, he smiled up large as soon as he realized it was Nelle. Never a dull encounter when

Nelle Callahan came to his counter. This lanky fellow with her though—some little tick 'round the back of his neck told him he'd seen him before. Couldn't place where. Couldn't place when. It'd come to him though. It always did. He ambled over, wiping down and spiffing up the true blue apron he favored. The couple who didn't behave like a couple selected and settled onto his red vinyl swivel stools. Naturally, Nelle took to swiveling first. Appraising fast at first spin.

"What's it all about, Albie? World treating you jake?" As soon as she'd shot her customary greeting to her customary coffee guy, Nelle winced at the jab stabbed by just murmuring the word *jake.* Jab dug around inside, where she hid how jaggedy felt.

The tall man who'd kept his damp fedora in place, noticed the lady's aplomb slip briefly out of place. The rotund coffee man sporting the twinkle to his eye, sparking the jut to his chin, noticed the notice.

"Same new, same new, Miss Nelle. Life be what you brew. And *you?*" Magruder's open glance both welcomed and scrutinized the fellow likewise giving him the once-over from under a soppy brim. "So what's it for you, bub?"

"Cup o' your strongest and a generous piece of lemon pie. I like taking my time with pie when conversing delicious with a captivating dame."

Magruder snorted.

Nelle ignored the men-sizing-up-men-moment. Tugged instead at wet tangles. Auburn tresses fell long and rambled loose, released from their scrunch in her trench. Flung from swung-back shoulders, they tousled their wayward way down the slope of her moss green sweater. She mocked a *get-a-load-of-this-guy* grin. Shot it full sweet force, Magruder's way.

Swiveling into the smug smile of the man sticking by the handle of Harry, Nelle relaxed into familiar aromas. Visibly. Her sensory perceptions? Always robust. A fresh brew percolated atop an old strain, Bing Crosby's "I Can't Begin to Tell You" crooning refrains from the lemon yellow Philco perched up high on the shelf behind the battered counter. Good place to begin a beguine.

"So why the smug smile? What do you need *me* to find, that an ingeniously slick palooka like you can't find, that the cops can't find? Huh, Harry?"

"Smile's 'cause I dig your style. You don't flinch much, Nelle. Knowing that, comes in handy should I ever need a clear-thinker edging out of a tight spot. I can tell you've known tight spots Callahan. And you've wriggled through."

"Fair enough. Now, what is it that you've lost or

misplaced or cheesed in the wrong nook of the wrong cranny's cupboard?"

Steamy black coffee in creamy porcelain mugs, with a pungent piece of lemon pie on a chipped blue plate, slid before the two main attractions at the Hill O' Beans' battered counter. Only other customer in the joint was the twitchy guy in the back booth with the newspaper who'd come in, just bell-tinkling moments before these two hidden-purpose stragglers.

Magruder slipped back to the sort of sorting of spoons and rattling of forks that made for background cover as he took in their jib jab jive. No grifter or button man was going to pull a flimflam on his pal Nelle, and that's what this bruno seemed. Unless or until he proved otherwise.

"I didn't *lose* it. I just can't find it."

"Is it there? Does it even exist?"

"I wouldn't have come rapping on your door, Miss Goody Gumshoe, nor be gulping black coffee with you now—Hey, this is *good,*" with an appreciative nod Magruder's way, "—if I didn't know *indeed* it was there. Well, somewhere. It's real alright, Callahan. Solid. True."

"You gonna tell me what *it* is so's I can have a shot at finding it all the better?" Nelle sipped slow, scanned his eyes, fast. There was something about those eyes. She'd never seen them stay in one place for too long. Not what you'd call shifty, but something—*assessing*. Assessing options before choosing which way to act rather than *react*. Like, should I steal third or stay on second? Yep, those vibes. Always makes sense relying on vibes. They convey you more than common sense, which is not at all what it's cracked up to be.

Below assessing eyes, firm lips spoke: "It's a will."

"*Will?* Well duck soup, Harry. Eggs in the coffee—no offense, Albie. Easy solution to your convolution. You need to find a lawyer's door for your rapping, not a detective's."

"I did."

"Why d'you need *me* then, Harry?"

"I went to his office. Found him behind his desk. A Mr. Gerald Dunnigan, Esquire. With two holes plugged where his Esquire used to be—his yap was closed. That mouthpiece just wasn't talking, Callahan."

~ ~ ~

Across the Hill O' Beans coffee shop, way back in the corner booth, sports pages rustled more than just the news that Philadelphia Phillies first baseman Eddie Waitkus was shot in Chicago by de-

ranged sports fan Ruth Ann Steinhagen.

The radio switched to a new tune, Evelyn Knight warbling "A Little Bird Told Me."

THE CHOCOLATE PEARL

Our tale of two trenches digs in, the better to counter what these two came in out of the rain for, at the battered cream counter of Albert Magruder's Hill O' Beans. Best cup o' joe a dark rainy night can brew. Sip the one you got or get yourself a refill...but then hop, skip or jump back onto your swell swivel stool. This hot tale is gettin' cool. The tall guy with the damp fedora is about to spill the beans 'bout what he's all about. But, you think we should we believe the guy? Do you?

~ ~ ~

As he unloaded a heap o' details, I heeded non-Harry closer than it looked like I was doing my heeding. Of course one eye darted to Newspaper Guy in the back booth every other rustle. Wasn't pretty how awfully immersed he was in that story about the wounded baseball player. Eddie Waitkus of the Phillies shot in Chicago by a deranged lady fan. *That guy won't round third no more.* You could hear his twitches rattle. Unless that was his nerves. Even with last month's news.

Then there was good old Albie in my peripherals. Shakin' his enormous iron fryer over his blackened back burners. Profusely. *Over—Slide—Over—Slide.* Only sound was grease on the sizzle. With no bacon and eggs orders up, this was grilling me 'round the edges as well. I listened and I heeded and I deliberated on all the sensations spining 'round me. I listened to this damp fedora fella who claimed—for now—he was no Tom nor Dick but preferred, for some precluded personal practicality, to dub himself a Harry. I heeded his claim he had a beef about a will. A will he and his dead lawyer couldn't readily get their hands on to handle. Paperwork's a bitch I tell ya. Yeah, I listened. And I heeded.

I heeded harder than I listened.

Wonder if anyone ever told un-Harry what a tell his left bushy eyebrow quirk is. Brown eyes. Akin to my prized mahogany. The kind that dig down inner-deep. He clenches too. Almost imperceptible 'round the jaw, but I percepted it. It's whenever he mentions...*Her*—

"My mother was not a normal mother as mothers go. We saw her come. We saw her go."

"Dances? Parties? That sort of fling?"

"Heavier on the fling." He pulled a deck of Luckies out of his inside suit pocket. *Pall Malls must just be for first impressions.* I saw what else skulked there. This guy rationalized he was full of surprises or wanted me to presume I thought so. Not that easy, bub, not that easy. He offered me one but I still had a good cup o' joe to be loyal to. Besides, I don't smoke, just sometimes pretend at pretending to. I declined. Kept the interrogation going friendly though. After all, this guy had more than lemon pie on his plate to chew.

"So, to your pop—your mother wasn't always true?"

"My father could've been *her* father. I imagine she desired more of a life than simply settling up silks and satins to what cushes a pampered wife."

"Vibrant is as vibrant does. You talk about your imaginings with other family much? You have brothers? Sisters? And what's this got to do with a bumped-off family retainer and your inability of acquiring due inheritance, Har? Ah, I can call you *Har*, right?"

I was right. Humpty Dumpty had to put his face back together again, lickety-split quick, when he forgot to react to his current claim to name. And here I was thinkin' this damp fedora fella had it on the ball. What's his story? *Everyone has a story.* That's why I'm listening. Heeding. Even over Albie's greasy smoke screen. Something's up. Something always is.

I'm Nelle Callahan and I sense trouble before it has a chance to trail me through darkened doorways. That's how I knew about my former squeeze, yet current business partner. Jake. That lousy crumbum. Last month at Hooligans, he chatted up a chirpy who had less in the noggin' than a bird brain and let loose feathers fly. Something too forward about how she fluttered cleavage against puffed-up chest—for an extra half-hour—gave her jig and jugs away. It wasn't too pretty how I responded. Jake returned with my bourbon and rye. I got up, socked him in the eye. Sat back down. Sipped. Sipped serious. Life's tough enough than to go wasting the best swigs of swell hootch. Besides, I had to think. Wasn't easy over Jake's drippy sputterings. Muttering protestations are seldom soft-spoke when only one of us holds the keys to all our clients' files. I kept my pocket secure. But enough about that. This supposed Harry is flapping his jaw harder and faster now.

~ ~ ~

"So I said to the guy, *What's the big grift?* There was something hinky, not quite right how he spilled his spiel," the man hunkered down as Harry leaned in to reveal.

Redirecting direct thoughts to make-believe Harry, Nelle shot back, "Wait—*what* guy? "

"I'm paying you to *pay attention*, Callahan. The guy who called and said he had my mother's ring. *The Chocolate Pearl.*"

TURKISH DELIGHT GONE SOUR

Our tale of two trenches counter the origins of a rare gem, bantering at the battered cream counter of the Hill O' Beans. Best cup o' joe a dark rainy night can brew. But you knew that. Go ahead. Sip along, keep your elbows plunked on the battered counter...but steer clear when the action heats up. You wouldn't want to get in the way. I've warned you.

~ ~ ~

"The Chocolate Pearl is RARE, Nelle! *That's* why you've never heard of it."

"Sure, sure, Harry-today. That's what they all say. *One-in-a-million.* Ain't none like it. Nowhere else in the whole wide world of views and vistas. That's the hubbub, huh, bub?"

"Actually, good deducing, Lady Gumshoe. But what's this 'Harry-today' rubbish?"

"Aw, applesauce. C'mon, man. You expect me

to buy in you're on the-up-and-up with all this? A sultan and a bequest, then a heisted carved chest doin' the swift swisheroo in *the Turkish Silk Market*? All to get to your missing mother's missing ring? Sounds pretty chic sheik to me, Ali Baba Boy. And who knows who *you* really are gonna turn out to be? I'm bettin' the pie and coffee tab you pulled 'Harry' outta your damp hat, Fedora Fella."

"Callahan, damnit, hear me out. Then take it all in. You'll see. I'm telling you what I'm telling you. *You'll see.*"

"Precisely what concerns me, Big Boy. Seeing it the way your spiel spills. It's sloppy. You got gaps a Duesenberg could spiral drive circles through. Thrice."

Chuckling a low rumble gaining high steam, with one eye peeled toward potential peals from the tiny silver bell over his coffee shop door, Albert Magruder topped their mugs with more strong joe and more soft thoughtfulness than he customarily poured counter customers. No saucer splash. No side-dribble slosh. Magruder took a breath. Cleared his throat. Cut straight in to their prattling din.

"Either of you ever hear of the Spoonmaker's Diamond?"

"Jeepers creepers," Nelle grimaced. "Is *everyone* dishin' exotic sparkle-tales today? Well go ahead,

Albie, spin *your* version of this fine fable if you think you're able...but then will you let me in on just *why* you're heating up that greasy ol' frying pan over and over? You got the heebie-jeebie jitters or are you tryin' to remember what all goes into some newfangled recipe you're hankering to try out on the ritzy swanks? Ain't any ham and egg orders 'round here. No takers on the stools but us and Nervous Neddie back in the back booth. Still rattling his attitude with his outdated newspaper. He's sippin'. He's thinkin' good and plenty about somethin', but he ain't chompin' on nothin'. Far as I can tell."

"Settle down, Callahan," the Harry-claimer cut in. His stare glared *dare*. Softened where it landed, tendering a melodramatic wink. Short order grin on the side. "So here's how it goes, kid: *I'm* the client here. *You're* supposed to be the discerning detective whose main role is *eager* to hear. Now *I'd* like to hear what our purveyor of percolation has to share. I'll wager dollars to doughnuts Mr. Magruder believes in my story."

Albert preened. Visibly.

Nelle groaned. Audibly. "Doughnuts? All this time I thought you were a pie-guy. *Sheeeesh.* Boys will be boys will be boys, though. You'd think testosterone would get tangled, the way you menfolk trip over seconding each other's notions." She stared down each. Scanned their bemused faces, catching the rustle-rustles ruminating out of the occupied booth in back. "Alright, alright already. Both you wisecracking bums stir me up this Diamond Spoon legend, then bring on the Chocolate Pearl chaser and we're either gonna have dessert or the fundamentals of a tale of a trail to finally follow."

The lemon yellow Philco flaunted valor up high, on the crammed shelf behind the cream-tiled, battered counter at the Hill O' Beans. Clinching its spot for twenty-three years, it had seen a lot, refrained a lot. At times, memorably so. At times, it seemed to tune into coincidences. But there's no real such thing as a coincidence, is there? The Philco kicked in now, accompaniment to the scene below:

> *Somewhere there's music.*
> *How faint the tune.*
> *Somewhere there's heaven.*
> *How high the moon.*
> *There is no moon about—*
> *when love is far away too.*

Proprietor Albie prepared to kick in to his tale

too. Harry-today leaned in to storied thoughts about to spill. Dark suited elbows pressed intensity over cream counter tiles. No distress for the meringue mess previously missing Harry's pie-hole.

Nelle gave in to listening in. As his avid audience swiveled tighter at his battered counter, Albert DeFonse Magruder regaled his tale, yet preserved peripherals upon one eavesdropper hanging loose in his back booth, still rustling rather than revealing what he'd come in for. Same cup o' joe for forty-five minutes perked way past suspicious. Stale as last month's news.

~ ~ ~

Albert began his beguine nice and serene.

"His love was far away...She was beautiful. Beautiful in the eyes of his heart, in the many roaming eyes of Istanbul."

His tale he remembered well. Magruder got around. Knew things. Random things, but not so random once you strung them together like a highly regarded necklace dangling between two more highly regarded velvet breasts.

"The young maiden Ozel had been taken away with her merchant family when the silk caravan made its usual route along the Meander River into Pamukkale. He knew she'd be back. Sugar, spice and everything nice was made for far more than a mere cup of chai. He had to catch her eye. Show well his worth when she returned."

Nelle realized she was succumbing to the web warmed by Albie's weave. A tapestry tale like he liked to tell, frequently threaded facted, fateful fiction. No telling in his telling which was which, but that's what made Albie's stories all the more engrossing. Easing into what mesmerizing does to mood and moment, she lingered a sideways look 'neath lush Maybellines at this Clyde dubbing himself a Harry. Holy cow, *he's eating this up.* Tough guy for soft tales. Maybe the mother ring rings true. *Chocolate Pearl, huh?* Mystery now. History in Turkey then. Gone missing once again. *Hmm.* There could actually be something to actually looking into this.

Magruder knew how to clutch an audience without even opening his clenched weathered palm—same way he'd developed his secret grounds, concocting the best cup of joe a dark, rainy night could brew. *Insight.* And insight muttered, murmured, sometimes even growled to the gut when trouble was brewing...or came struttin' its stuff down a dark, rainy street. But for now, *there were only these two.* Comfortable at his counter. Comfortable in their banter. A guy with a mug vaguely familiar, needing his new pal with the pretty nose to sniff out what was on the up and up. Needing her more, he figured, for how swell Nelle could slice and deduce shadows.

Indeed, Nelle Callahan mastered more than a fair shake from any skill she decided to hone in on. Magruder fathomed all along that her detective dexterity was some sheen of a smoke-screen swirling over some deeper involvement, but he hadn't figured the particulars out on that one yet. And Nelle wasn't telling.

She kept silent like the clock on the wall kept ticking. As did insight. *Louder. Louder.*

Albert Magruder's insight sensed trouble. Imminent trouble. But a story is a story, is a story—and this tale was off on a rousing good tell.

~ ~ ~

"What's that? His name? It's *Coskun*," Magruder replied. "It means *enthusiasm,* and a poor man enriched with a beautiful woman certainly has plenty of that, doesn't he, Harry?"

Magruder kept up his spiel as the nodding man kept down his coffee, savoring.

"He let spirit manifest his ardent desire for the merchant's lovely daughter. One day, walking by the rubbish heap of Egrikapi, a glimmer caught canny Coskun's eye. He reached in. Dug around. Pulled out a colossal bewitching stone. An alluring stone. One that rendered him the market deal of the day, I might say. And then Coskun bartered one of the most magnificent diamonds Turkey or the world had ever seen through all of antiquity, to the local spoonmaker for three of his most finely crafted wooden spoons."

"That's it, Magruder? *Three lousy spoons?* How's a guy gonna charm the dame he's hot for when he's so lame that he opts for silly *spoons?* Guy's got no game."

Nelle laughed. Hard. Her chuckle rose round to howls, reverberating the room for three men's delighted ears. Some pairs that were supposed to be listening. One pair that was not.

"Maybe he'll open a kebab restaurant, Har," she sputtered. "Serve the sultan something bold beyond the pale. Be pulled into service as chief sampler-of-cuisine at Topkapi Palace. He'll be sure to get the girl along the way, since his magic carpet obviously rides to delicious success. Imagine hues of happily ever after as suns rise and set 'cross the Bosporous. Pretty heady stuff, huh? Why, the next thing ya know, they up the ante, go into caravan cahoots. Smuggle chocolate pearls—"

"Put a lid on it, Nelle. I want to hear the rest of

this story. Mr. Magruder, pay no attention to my tin pan alley detective mucking up myths with mazes. Would you kindly continue?" Harry-today turned to his left. Swiveled like he meant it. Glared down the dame getting his goat. He hated when someone got his goat, even when they were kidding around.

Nelle winked into the stare of fake-Har's dared glare. Slow. Deliberate. Just this side of inside sultry. She tilted her comeuppance along with her moss green snug sweater. Wiggled wide her shoulders too. Hoped her reactions were driving this fella a little crazy. He was gettin' to her and she didn't need to be gotten to. What she needed was to stay sharp. Real sharp. Somethin' wasn't summing up the score on this fellow's up-and-up.

~ ~ ~

The silver bell didn't ring twice, not even once, when the Hill O' Beans' door splinter-smashed open. Hadn't a tinkle of a chance. The hoodlum hefting the handle harked business. And from the hip hep of his hustle, he damn well meant it. Quick. Hasty quick. Danger-in-the-gut quick. The fellow in the back booth with the old newspaper about the baseball player done wrong? Heck, he left his post, post-haste. Headed to the Men's. In nuttin' flat.

Magruder's Turkish delight tale? It forfeited both tempo and timing. This was the minute the hour had gone sour.

Making his way straight away to the stocky man behind the battered counter, Tough Guy thumped his chest. Twice. Brayed the way *diabolical* sounds when it's divulging it holds all the cards in a loaded deck of a crooked game. His ugly puss wrangled eyeball to eyeball into Albert Magruder's face, who flinched not. "Got a message to deliver, Alb. You keep stirrin' the street up 'gainst payin' protection like you're s'posed to be doin' 'round here, youse gotta pay anudder price. A higher price. A learn-a-lesson-better price. So how you want your lesson taught, Magruder? Out here in front of the local joe and pie loiterers? Or do we take the tutorin' I'm gonna learn ya, out back?"

The Harry-moniker-man wasn't a man who liked a swell story interrupted. Especially a story he gleaned was well worth its way to substantiating *his* story. Well sure, he figured Magruder doled deliberate liberties with his delivery, but he expected this continuing saga of the Spoonmaker's Diamond to wend its way to his own Chocolate Pearl's mystery of history. This dope duping the story-telling coffee man was way in the way. He reached for his pocket bulge.

Tough Guy had absolutely no time for pocket-graspers slowing the purpose of *his* purpose. One sharp whack from the hoodlum's knack with the back of a flair-handled Python knocked the pie eater's snub-nosed pistol clean. It spiraled. Spun itself dizzy. Tough Guy shot once into the Hill O' Beans' linoleum, punctuating the statement he had the floor. Powder burns and epithets stunk up the air. Pissed past irritability, he kicked the guy's pistol clear. Bonked the bent-over gent with the pie on his tie. Impact to noggin? Hard. Extremely hard. Hard enough the guy hit the floor and saw cartoon birdies chirpin' ring around the rosies over his head.

Burly prowess pivoted. Veer and sneer shot clear to Magruder. Time to give what the Boss sent him for giving. A cooperation scare. In his line of work, folks should cooperate more, they should.

Not to be left out of a good floor show, Nelle stepped right in to center stage action. Nailed the hothead shooter. Deftly. Clean shot down his inside upper thigh with her Colt DS, Detective's Special. "Whoo Hoo! Target practice near the family jewels! Well, story that gem, boys," she smirked, as Magruder let sizzling grease from his iron frying pan plan fly. Welts and wails, wails and welts mutated the cringing mass of a not-so-handy hired gun into a seriously scalded, marked man. Clunk! Conked decisively in his final round down, with the hot and heavy dripping pan. Albie always sported a prepared plan.

Nelle hooted over Albie's able encore, "This bub's not so hard-boiled anymore, is he, Alb? But hey, we're gonna have to put the skids under him, y'know? Backroom, ya think? Tell ya what, I'll be back, help you in a jiff—but I got two quick somethins I gotta take care of first."

Leaning over the alternate floor sprawl, the one with dampened fedora, crushed spirit and inherited treasure to *re*find, the one masquerading a moniker of Harry midst a murky night, Nelle Callahan hissed harsh her whisper, softened though, with carmelized eyes, "Don't *ever* pull your heater unless you're prepared to *use* your heater. Ya got that, Harry?"

She whirled to the cool-as-a-cucumber-in-a-coffee-shop percolating proprietor. "Albie, this slight interruption to your first-rate enchantment of storytelling has me kinda late for a pressing date. Okey dokey if I use your phone?" With a nod towards the greasy crumbum floor mess, she pinched her nose. "Promise. I'll help you with Stinky here, soon's I get back." Nelle hustled past empty back booths to the short paneled hallway beyond. Called over her shoulder, "We all know he ain't goin' nowhere fast."

"Suit yourself, Nelle. We know you always do," Magruder chuckled, leaned down. Selected limbs to pick and choose from. Heaved the heap hailing as Harry back on his feet. Hollered down the hallway, "You can use the pay phone on the wall in the hall or make yourself more comfortable back in my office. Millie surprised me with a leather swivel chair. Check it out, Nelle, she's a beaut. And Millie still is too!"

Nelle grinned large. *Ain't love grand?* She'd introduced Albie to Millie Marcine Haversham after a square-deal case a few months back. The widow Haversham was one peach not having a fruitful time at the time. The two femmes hit it off despite a generation of difference they split together. Working together, they'd put the kabosh on the frame-up a local syndicate was hanging on Millie's son Jimmy. Poor kid was doin' time for a crime someone in Joey Adonis' repulsive gang had committed. That jerk Joey? He was never no nice guy.

Funny, Joey's gang was poppin' up on her nemesis list an awful lot lately. And the boys who played rough in that gang were goddamn awful with how they lunged and leered their rough. Either they were very prolific at being awful, or some grubby game was afoot. A detective never clueless, Nelle'd bet her own brown suede fedora some new, ornery game was kickin' up its nasty. Maybe worse than their usual kinds of vicious. And that was plenty nasty past plenty.

When something seems not right—it isn't. *Illusions are never what they're swirled up to be.* And Joey Adonis, though over-the-hill and pretty much crippled cranky now—both in poor physicality and lousy leadership skills—had dirty secret doings a long time ago involving her deceased mother. Well, so she'd heard in hush-hush whisper-speak. Canaries down the docks and words on the street both warble their tunes...when you listen good, or ask better. Nelle intended to do more of each, once she cleaned up her current spinning plates. *What she was trying to doing now.*

Passing the wall phone, she automatically jiggled the bottom black return cup. Never know when you need to spare a buddy a loose dime. Empty. She hotfooted her intent towards Albie's back office. Privacy for private eyes was an *under-stood*, no matter if you were calling your mother or the milkman or the D.A. in L.A., or, in a very grave situation, a dirt-digger. The looker detective who never gave herself glim for glam, sighed. There was never gonna be any calling *her* mom. Angel had tragically died, heaving birth and heritage to her only daughter, Nelle.

Folks 'round these parts still fondly hailed the renowned raven-haired beauty, Angel Towse Callahan, as *The Charm and Courage Bootlegger*. Legend linked lore to her allure. She was one tough, tender, admirable lady for sure. One who brung business to the Bay—stokin' up pocket-open broke Depression days to un-idle fishing boats her service called into extra-service. Bootlegging Narragansett Bay. Angel Towse, or *Angel Tough*, as she answered to proudly, was vigorously loved. Vitally loved. Her effervescence tip-topped a room, charming it to dance a jig or tear up the Charleston, right alongside her. Nelle yearned to have been able to love her now "guardian Angel" back then too. The Towse surname translated to "Tough" in the rough and tumble English countryside where Angel grew that way too. Precisely what she passed on to namesake Nelle. Nelle *Towse* Callahan. *To be tough. All ways, all days.* You never know what's coming at you. *You just never do.*

~ ~ ~

The arm in the pale yellow and blue madras sleeve thrust like a walloped ground rule double out the Men's Room door. Strong grip came with pale yellow. Grip clamped hard over Nelle's right arm. Grip didn't pull Nelle in, rather pushed her out. Out the back door. Out into the back alley. The rain had cleared. The alley smelled fresh. The guy who came with the grip, didn't. And he was breathing fast, hard and close. Nelle made a mental note to ask Albie again what ingredients went into his secret coffee recipe.

Callahan let her arm appear stuck tight in its grim, smelly grip. Went limp. Swung around quick. Yanked out, under and away from Mr. Arrow Shirt, seamlessly. Freed herself as well from his crummy breath. She pointed her index finger with raised thumb to her armed pocket, making a point of who he was messin' with. She had no time for his jostling jive. She was on a mission to make a phone call about a mission. Chief said she he had to reconnoiter with Moe. Today.

The guy stepped back. Thought quick. Advanced forward, anyway.

She gave the bub the quick-over before he fancied any more fancy step-outs. The fellow actually looked harmless. More shook up than posing any diligent threat. And he cradled his other arm over his chest. Like he was holding something in. A sad sap wantin' to know if she'd be a buddy and spare him a dime? Too bad the phone cup had been empty. Mebbe Albie gave him coffee on the house and he only read discarded newspapers? *Hey, who knew?*

She would. Once she got to the bottom of what was up. Besides, she had to check in with Moe. In a hurry past her late.

"So what's the matter with you, bub? Can't you just tap a lady on the shoulder? Offer her some *Pardon me while I make your acquaintance* scintillating chit chat?"

The guy looked down. As did Nelle. She scrutinized black cleated shoes, not the normal brogues or wingtips usually observed around town. He firmed his stance around his determination. Made up his mind to start jabbering. Good gosh! This bub articulated a roller coaster of a blue streak, like time wasn't whooshing any leeway on his side. Like it was the bottom of the ninth and the Ump was crookeder than what the scoreboard was adding up to.

He looked her solemn in the eye though, for all his fast pitchin'. Blurted, "I had to meet you, Miss Callahan. Talk to you. Get your help. Fast. *Real* fast. My time of the season's running out, ya see. A mutual chum told me where I might find you. He said you'd know how to handle it—"

She cut him off like the squiggly tips she hated at

the end of green beans. Concise, precise. "You ever hear about the invention called a telephone? Think about knockin' on a door that might open? Making one of those appointment things?"

Surprisingly, the guy reciprocated just the opposite of how Nelle's diatribe usually jostled potential adversaries off guard. He chipped up his jaw. Swaggered back his shoulders. Declared straight out, but in a low voice meant only for the lady before him, "You see, Miss Callahan, I didn't want folks recognizing me."

"I almost didn't, without the rustled newspapers you usually sport across your face. You a slow reader, bub? That Eddie Waitkus wounded baseball player story is over a month old."

There was stillness. Then came a soft, thoughtful voice. Voice lifted just below a quizzical brow. "You knew what was featured on the sports pages from all the way over where you were at the counter?"

"No hocus pocus to that focus, bub," Nelle said. "Sports pages come with pictures for palookas done lookin' up the little numbers in the box-scores and standings. Some of their kind don't take kindly to a whole lot of words. Hurts their heads or somethin'." Her laughter bubbled as mirth personified. It righted all the wrong angles of the dejected alley.

"Yeah, I recognized who the story was about."

Another thought impacted breathing break. Then the voice again. A little resigned. A lot subdued. "Listen, I know it's dim and dark in this alley here, Miss Callahan, but I want you to know I wouldn't try any funny business. Will you look *closer*? Will you take a real good gander at me? Tell me what you see, or who you think you see?"

Nelle had a hot hankering for telling this gripper guy off instead. She wasn't scared, this was just getting tedious. And taking time. But she looked. Occupational habit. She looked.

And she let low a long, keen whistle. The whistle circled several galvanized garbage pails, picked up pace, boomeranged back. "Holy Mackerel! *YOU'RE Eddie Waitkus!*"

Eddie Waitkus led off first. Spilled his beans fast. He knew what he'd come for. Nowadays he was the kind of man who didn't appreciate gawking, who cared none for pity. Neither advanced his current position. He played first base for the Philadelphia Phillies. Well he *did*—

"Here comes my story, ma'am. And I thank you in advance for the time I pressed you into hearing me out." Eddie took a breath, deep and sustaining. "We were back in Chicago, you see, where I used to play. After the game and a little celebrating with the fellas, I returned to the Edgewater Beach Hotel. Late. Wanted to hit the mattress. Was a helluva game, Miss Callahan. Helluva game. So first things first, I kicked off my cleats, then right away, there's this rap-rap-rapping on my door. Bellhop's there with a folded-over note. I tipped the kid a Hamilton. Skimmed the note a perfunctory read. Some broad wanted to see me. In her room. Said it was very important. See, I used to play in Chi-town and well, who knew who maybe I used to know from then. Like, who knew?"

"Eddie, I actually know how your story ends up. I'm mighty sorry about what happened to you—and now, well—I sure wanta hear how it played out. But listen, slugger, you're lookin' green around your gills. Howzabout you take a load off?"

Nelle prodded an empty garbage can nearer with her foot, then leaned against the Hill O' Beans' back door. Eddie overturned it. Hunkered down. Spouted out his tale. He never broke stride. He was still clutching his shirt though. But Nelle wasn't about to interrupt again. She knew a man makin' a line drive to spit out what he was on base for—should be heard out.

"Note was signed *Ruth Anne Burns*. Tell ya the truth, I couldn't recollect any Ruth, but get this—she asked if I would hurry up to her room. Said she had something important to tell me. 'Member, I said it was already late? So's I phoned her room, had to be around eleven, little after. She tells me she'd already gone to bed and would have to get up and get dressed. Asked me to wait half-an-hour, then come knock on her door. Hell, I'm curious now. So—"

"So you did."

"I did. Most brainless, boneheaded thing I ever did too. She opens the door. Tall drink of water, but young, scraggy, kinduva pinched in face, like she was a bellyacher. Came to me *what the hell'd I let myself in for*? But dumb dame damage done, I'm already there. Dogged tired though. She didn't say anything. Nope, nothin' at all. Just stood there at the door, givin' me this moony look. I saw a chair, three glasses. Across the room. Like maybe a little party. So I pushed past her. When I got there, two of the glasses were empty. Chair wasn't. I took it and started to ask her what this was all about. What was so important I had to come see her?"

"That's *when*?"

"Yep, Miss Callahan. When she kinda got— juiced. You know, electrified. She pirouetted. Like a wild whirlygig thing. Stowed something shiny on the desk by the door. Then she kinda flounced or pranced over to the closet. Half pretty, half scary as shit. Cocks her head t'wards me and swings her long hair to swaying back and forth, you know, like a pendulum does. She teased out, all singsongy, 'I have a *surprise* for you, Eddie.' I'm no horndog, Miss Callahan, but a guy gets more than his curiosity up sometimes in hotel rooms. Uh, you know what I mean."

Nelle smirked, patted his good arm. "Yes, I've heard tell of horndogs and hotels, Mr. Waitkus. G'head, but then I'm askin' Albie to rustle you up a roast beef sandwich. When's the last time you ate?"

Waitkus cut her short, no appetite for delay. "Wait. I got something real important to ask of you, Miss Callahan. Something our mutual friend said you'd know the way as to the *how* to fix right for me. So, you see, I can't eat much, I can't relax 'til I get this whole dumb sob-story out but...I'm not the boo hoo blubbery type. No crying in my cleats here. The broad was an out-and-out whacko."

"How so, Eddie?" Nelle knew what the newspapers reported, but she discounted black and white when true colors were standing up right before her to be read.

"Well hell, Nelle...you read the papers, you know what's next. She fetches a .22 caliber rifle out of her closet. She points it at me. Tells me to get out of her posh chair and go stand in front of the window. She opens her eyes then. Big. To jumbo-size. Then she shimmies her stuff, blows me this sexy puss-kiss and purrs, 'For two years, Eddie, you've been bothering me and now you're going to die.' Then, she shot me."

"In the chest?"

"Upper right field line. Hotel dick and Doc happened to be in the hallway. Right there. Right then. *Imagine that.* They arrested Crazy Ruth in nothin' flat. Hauled me into an ambulance *just happening* to be out front too. Turns out the big buck tip she gave the bellhop to get me the note was nuttin' up to how I'd subsidized the kid. I'd autographed a ball for him too. Later, when he got off duty, he shows up at the hospital. A real good kid was this Johnny Kozel. He fills me in some more, 'bout his buddy from Room Service delivering her two whiskey sours and a daiquiri. The bud stood in the hall. Watched her down one of the whiskies. All in one gulp, just standin' there. Then she stiffed him on the tip. Lucky for me, huh? Those hotel boys put their heads together and smelled somethin' rotten at the edges of the Edge-water. Reported it right away to the front desk. Quick-thinkers there, those boys, goin' the distance, I'll tell you."

Nelle grinned, but tight-lipped, drifted in closer. Asked, "Eddie, may I?" and to Waitkus' watchful nod, she traced the spot where he showed her he was shot. "Damn tough break as tough breaks go, Eddie. So...now...now you're out of the Show?"

"No, ma'am. That's why I'm here. Why we're havin' this back alley talk in this crazy world we try to do our best stuff in. *I want back in.* The bullet pierced a lung, got caught short in one of the muscles in my back. Mebbe the rhomboid. I've had two operations to plug those predicaments. Both Doc Leeve and my trainer Wally prescribed some physical therapy maneuvers to restrengthen my rehabilitating. That's really *why* I'm here. If I don't get back in by the end of this season, I could be all washed up. No amount of sensation nor sympathy is going to give me good field position."

"You came to *me* for this?"

"Yes indeedy, Miss Callahan. Was told by a fellow ball player you have a winning way with folks who hang out in clubby, high places. Was told you can do a bang up job discreetly, so there's no red tape, fuss, muss or newshawker hoopla. This all came from a solid source. One I never question, when he starts pointing out the salt of his salient points. We both know him swell. I played with him one season in Chicago and he sorta alluded he's in some kind of tip-off affiliation with you—Moe Berg."

Nelle rolled back her shoulders. Shook out her auburn tresses. Cursed quick and quiet. "Of all the ballplayers in all the stadiums trudging off all the playing fields, it has to be that damn Moe Berg, huh?" She sighed, knowing already she was batter-boxed in without even leavin' the dugout. "Tell you what, Eddie, I'm gonna look into this, do some creative cogitatin' on it and...well, I'll pass on to Moe any informing of what comes of it. Right now, I've got a case on my plate and a serving dish on the side to clean up first. This career concern of yours though? It's got *Timing* with a capital *T* all over it though, right?"

"Right as rain, Miss Callahan, like tonight's...like tomorrow's, but that's about as far as I can wait. Doc Leeve swore I can heal this up right and still get September in. So ya see, I've gotta get back on the active roster...but my manager's doing a dodge and murmur thing."

Nelle knew all about dodges and murmurs. And Nelle knew in her gut—where the best impressions speak their better minds—Eddie Waitkus was a straight-up guy not leanin' into lookin' for trouble. Only *Trouble* with a capital *T* went out and found him.

A flatfoot pal, now the D.A. in L.A., had recently been calling Nelle, as he did on holes in certain cases he shot the breeze with her through. He hypothesized other slants of this story from where he'd been working the case of a deranged Hollywood fan angle. Ruth Ann Burns was really one Ruth Catherine Steinhagen who'd had the same stalker crazed crush on movie star Alan Ladd. Their discovery led, to another ballplayer as well, Peanuts Lowrey of the Chicago Cubs. The D.A. deduction? This looney evidently had a pining away penchant, falling hard as hailstones for men out of reach.

Over a series of late night phone calls, Nelle had back and forthed and forthed and back with him on theories. He asked her to poke holes in the plausible story 'til they couldn't find them anymore. 'Til they held the right light. Her colleague's pro-fesssional conjectures got stuck and concerned over some odd evidence—a bizarre shrine built and com-piled from photos, clippings and collected memora-bilia erected in a puny walkup. When she asked him to describe the room's overall appearance, her colleague told her there was nothing else there but two changes of clothes, a book on Lithuanian culture and cans and cans of baked beans. *The beans were pyramid-stacked, over an array of sports sections culled from regional dailies. A simple metal can-opener on the side,* is how her pal, D.A. Dale, summarized the findings of his investigation. Stumped on the beans link to the foreign-affairs reading material, he powwowed with Nelle's shrewd deductions. Amassed long-distance phone bills courtesy of the state of California. At the same time, Dale attempted to amass more than deductions back up with Nelle, but that storyline she wasn't buying into. Friends they'd remain. They concurred enough incriminating evidence existed to corroborate their tandem cross-country theories. But to connect them, they'd need more info to fill gaps. Otherwise, they only had illuminations to flash judge and jury ways.

"Eddie," Nelle asked, plugging a longshot hunch. "Where are you from, originally, and did you go to church with your folks?"

"Funny question, but Moe said to trust any low hoppers you grounded my way, Miss Callahan." He grinned tender, remembering being the rangy kid who played catch with Pop after services 'til Ma called 'em in for Sunday dinner. "Boston. I'm from Boston, ma'am, and yeah...we were regular Lithuanians. Roman Catholics. Held tight to our rosaries every Sunday." He scratched his head, reached in his back pocket. Pulled out his folded, true blue Phillies cap. Smoothed it, then planted it firmly, back where it belonged. "That help any? And do ya think I stand a prayer of a chance?"

"Might." Nelle grinned. She hated loose ends, even when they were someone else's. She'd call Dale later. Later...whew, she was running pretty late for later. "Hey, Eddie, I genuinely want to help you out. This is way more than a foul ball or a bummer Ump's call. I'll see what I can do. Not super promising anything, but I'm a solid baseball fan, I'm gonna give this its fair shake."

Waitkus hung his head, went silent. To his credit, where the lady in the keen green sweater couldn't see it, his eyes misted 'round their corners. Past the recent remembrance of his pop, he could now hear his ma: *Good folks are the best rewards we slide into home plate to score.* Then he straightened up. Went all business. Brusqued away errant emotion. Struck out his hand to fair shake hers. "I intend to pay you, Miss Callahan. Whatever your detectivizing fees are these days, plus expenses...but past that, lady, this is my *world*, this means the world. How'm I *ever* gonna, y'know, *really* thank you?"

Nelle looked amused, placed her slim hand quick and easy into Eddie's offered paw. Shook it firmly and kept her glimpse into seeing this sporting fellow's soft side to herself. Yeah, Eddie was alright. "Tell ya what? You get back into fielding practice before games, howzabout you whiz extra balls into the upper decks at kids hangin' over the wall with what looks like their pop's too big glove? *Deal?*"

Waitkus popped a soft fist into his palmed hand, curved in like a mitt. Beamed. Gave the same soft fist a playful punch to Nelle's upper shoulder. "You gotta deal, Callahan. But you'll see more from me. I'll think of something. I always do." He shifted off the trash can, righted it, dusted his rump. Turned to go. "Won't be keepin' you no more then. Moe knows how to find me. And I'll find a way to express genuine gratitude to you again, one good day, I do expect. Watch for it."

He tipped his cap. Hoofed ahead towards the damp, darkened alley running behind the shadows of the buildings on State Street, that fate street. His tread was lighter. His shoulders caught a lucky breeze where they'd been stuck in the funk of his slump. Eddie Waitkus had places to go. Places mapped with hope turned to trust to *absolutely* get there, to round the bases right again.

Much as sharp instinct urges every elite ball-player's hunches and judgements to react to a precise moment in time, Waitkus spun around. Right there, right then. What he took a good long gander at was the stance of detective Nelle Callahan. Poised, irrefutable—as if she was simply, thus strongly, waiting for that clear cut, instinctive moment too, the one where he turned around.

"I don't get it," he cupped his hands 'round his mouth and hollered back down the alley. His voice angled off wet trash cans. Reverberated intended echoes. "I mean, I'm appreciative as all get out, Callahan, but...*why'd* you do it? Why'd you just say you'd help me—no more questions asked, no more negotiations made?" He laughed a quick laugh, this dark-haired dreamboat from above-the-folds of American heroes' newspaper pages. "Don't change your mind or anything, but will you tell a wondering fellow the *why* behind your nimble-be-quick thinking?"

"*You* said it," Nelle raised her voice, acknowledging his need to know, but remained in place, as still as the night.

"Something *I* said convinced *you*—that solid?"

"Yep. You said she was a whacko. Rifle in the closet. Since there's no such thing as a coincidence, a source I could readily rely on had already inform-ed me—that shiny object was a knife stowed on the front desk. A concealed knife she'd planned to use on you. To kill you. You blew that opportunity when you blew on by her. She was preemptive enough to have a rifle, fetchable from her closet though. In a suicide note not needed—for there was no suicide—she said she'd planned to kill herself right after killing you. Living under the strain of not getting who she wanted meant she simply, thus strongly, wanted to kill off that strain. You know what that makes you, Eddie?"

"No, Callahan. What?"

"A victim. Tough as you are, Baseball Guy, you were a victim. My life's dedicated to the whacko not winning in the final inning over the victim. Not once. Not ever."

Eddie went quiet down his end of the alley.

"Good enough for you, Mr. Waitkus?"

"Great enough for me, Miss Callahan. You're aces up, lady," Eddie Waitkus soft-hollered.

He hustled his cleats in the rain-washed alley to where the rickety grey lamppost beckoned with more light, but he felt he'd just received illumination enough to see him through any dark season.

BOTTOM OF THE INNING

Light at the end of a dark alley is a good thing. So is helping the Victims beat the Whackos when they come to cheat the odds. But loose ends? Man, they're killers. You'll see. Oh yeah, you'll see.

~ ~ ~

Nelle Callahan took a certain pride in watching the rising shoulders of Eddie Waitkus as his shadow diminished. In her line of work, boosting shadows' shoulders was a big deal.

First baseman Eddie Waitkus could feel in his healing bones that he'd be back on first and rounding bases again. He wanted to yell *Good night!* to the world just so he could wake up bright to what tomorrow's scoreboard might have on deck. *"Good night, Mrs. Calabash, wherever you are!"* he belted out in a passable Jimmy Durante impression. Waitkus splashed fancy footwork into the pool of light the rickety grey lamp post shimmered over pain-washed, rain-washed State Street.

He raised his Phillies cap high, gave it too, its fair shake. The session with Callahan had been a solid hit. Now? Now it was time for second things first. Hop a train, make tracks out of this shadowy city by the Bay. *Blue skies, nuttin' but blue skies*, was what he wanted comin' in his new tomorrows. He'd hear good stuff, from his former teammate, old Cubs' catcher Moe Berg, as to what Callahan could pull off. He was sure of that. Gut-perceptions are legit. So, off to Philly and his old Blue Jays team, now newly dubbed the Phillies because of some fan outrage. Geeez, Eddie had had it with fan outrage, boy oh boy, had he. Nothin' was stopping him now.

Wait. The Bat! Damn it. He forgot the bat. Now he had to backtrack. Must've left it back in the back booth, back at the Hill O' Beans. Yeah, must've been during his dashaway when that numbskull hood gusted in with the wind to shake down the coffee shop guy. Decent sort, that coffee guy. Good thing Callahan was in the joint when trouble brewed half past robust. *And yeah, that was some good coffee.* But the owner, Magruder, looked like he could careen himself out of any trouble that tinkled his bell. For an old codger, the guy was sharper than a fielder's choice. Knew which way he'd react, is how Eddie saw it.

But the bat. He had to go back for the bat.

~ ~ ~

The bat was a stunner. Not your run-of-the-bases Louisville Slugger. Had to be an A.J. Reach Deluxe Burly. Sported a unique green tint with a taped up handle. It was hand-turned and had a sweet spot etched with a player swinging only the stuff grandslams are made for.

When the shooting troubles shook up Chicago, making the roster troubles lock down Philly, Eddie speculated it smart to have his contract looked into and looked over. Didn't want to get hung up in anybody's loopholes. So he went out on the town to find the best mouthpiece to speak his mind. In the city of Philadelphia, that means a *Social Register*-type, a sole-practice guy emerging from the best uppercrust families with the ability to score substantial reach past mere wealth and power. Pun intended, Eddie Waitkus liked to cover all his bases. As fate poured out, he chanced upon one Jerry Dunnigan at McGillin's Olde Ale House, a popular watering-hole in business since the Liberty Bell got cracked up. Eddie took the solid history of the venue as a worthy sign. Proving a good harbinger as well, was Dunnigan, who like most of Philadelphia, was an avid sports fan. The attorney-at-law recognized the baseball-player-not-at-bat while ordering the house brew, McGillin's Genuine Lager. Hailed him over. As the two shot the breeze, Eddie spelled out his needs. Bottlenecks clinked. They set up a meeting in Dunnigan's office. Next morning. Ten sharp.

Eddie arrived early. Killed time with a good time over peach pie and a dishy peach at the dinette across the street. Was settling up his tab, adding in his autograph with a dreamy wink for Zelda, the peachy waitress, when two black-suited, flinty looking guys tripping over themselves charged down the limestone steps across the street. Under the carved gold-leaf sign swinging *Dunnigan Esquire, Dunnigan Esquire,* Eddie sensed unjustifiable trouble. Since he'd genuinely liked Jerry, about as much as he'd liked last night's McGillin's genuine lager, he bolted across the street, bounded the not to be taken for granite steps two-at-a-time. Breezed into the sedate marble hallway. Found Dunnigan's ornate open door. Found Dunnigan. On the floor.

Kneeling, a disheveled Dunnigan was sorting skewered documents under smattered desk accoutrements. The great legal man was cursing more like a sailor than *Social Register* gentry. He iterated and reiterated, *Client privilege,* in repeated curt murmurs to Eddie's rapid-fire *What the hell just happened?* queries. Eddie got the points of Dunnigan's despairing point, quit asking and shut up. He hunkered down to hands, knees and the task at hand. Made progress quietly alongside his frustrated attorney. The two floor foragers culled and collated all they could deem as unruined. In the process they formed a respecting, respectable team. Eddie set stacks of salvaged paperwork across Dunnigan, Esquire's expansive oak desk, while the beleaguered barrister took his seat behind it. He motioned the big league ballplayer to do the same, indicating the navy blue wingback they'd just righted.

Dunnigan sighed deep and shook off all outward appearances of angst. Composed himself, to delve into detailed business as usual. Removed his mind from his messes. Eddie's own recent scrape with dangers from the unexpected, deduced, dollars to doughnuts, it must be a pretty unpleasant scenario the elder gent was seeking to avoid. Both men acknowledged each other's thoughts through not acknowledging. Focused instead on clauses, paragraphs and potentialities spelled out in the Philadelphia Phillies franchise's boilerplate contract. The attorney got the ballplayer to see his precise point, where his finger tapped out particular attention to the morals and "ability to play" clauses.

The re-dignified Dunnigan advised amicably, "Waitkus, get back into the game sooner than later, so *no funny stuff slides by first.*"

Eddie thanked him. Joked back, "Sure Jerry...but you *can't* slide into first."

Dunnigan chuckled. Deliberated. Decided. Raised his palm to pause their banter.

The office door had been closed and locked during their collating and conference time. Still, Dunnigan stood. Paced solicitously around glass fragments and ink bottle stains dotting and crossing the lines of his black and gold Aubusson. Deliberated some more. He turned back the massive brass handle on his solid oak door. Arched his balding head into the empty hallway. Deserted. Still, he peered to the left. Apprehensively, he peeked to the right. Like a kid not wanting to get run over on a busy street with his mother nowhere in sight. He exhaled. Capaciously. Swiveled his awareness back to Eddie, stretched out his hand. Graciously.

Eddie rose, returning the firm handshake. Gave the tense legal gent due process—a compassionate look. One that looked right through to another's psyche. He saw capable, yet agitated attorney eyes, registering distress. Jagged fear and foreboding registered too. Eddie knew the look. Same he'd sported when a rifle got fetched out of a hotel closet instead of a coat hanger.

"Hey, Jer, anything I can do for you anytime I'm in town, rather than out of town, you just holler, hear?" Eddie said, hoping a consolatory tone might diminish despair.

Dunnigan acknowledged with an open eye-to-eye nod edging out his daze. Thumped Waitkus on the back. "Oh, you're a good sort, Eddie. Despite your unfortunate circumstances, I'm quite glad we've had this opportunity to meet. I certainly look forward to seeing you getting back into sports action again. We're due for a pennant. We always are."

Eddie leveled the nod. Tipped his ball cap. Sauntered past the open ornate door, into the—

"Wait, *wait*, Waitkus!" Gerald Dunnigan, Esquire commanded. He'd made up his mind as his own inner judgement called. The stuff of guts speaks loudest. The imperious tone emanating from the legal mouthpiece was *Decision* speaking full force. "You say 'anytime you're in town' and you're actually out of town a lot. Then you come back in. Away games and—"

"Yep," Eddie cut in, relieved to watch distress take a breather, though not sure where Dunnigan's fair wind was drifting. "What do you need, sir?"

Something about being stuck down and out made a guy not want to see another guy stand too idle with his hands dredging his pockets the same dismal way.

"Ah, without inquiring into definitive questions, would you bestow me a great favor by taking something along with you...something that would blend right into the kind of baseball travels you do out of town and back into town...just to...ah, keep it safely out of my office for a short time?"

"What kind of something?"

"A baseball bat."

"Baseball bat?"

"Baseball bat."

"That's it?"

"That's it. I've assured a concerned client I'd...*ah*, keep it out of harm's way."

"Harm's way, you say?"

Dunnigan held a steady bead on the character of Eddie's eyes. Clinched confirmation. Reached into the umbrella stand behind the brass rack sporting a spare sport coat, checkered tie and a Burberry trench. Wrenched out an impressive ash log, much as Arthur extracted Excalibur from stone. Lifting and brandishing the impressive bat, he couldn't help admiring it once more. Extended it vertically, tossing it into the small gap between the two men now...playing ball.

Reflexively, Eddie caught it mid-center.

"The harm's local," Dunnigan responded, grasping the bat by making a fist that wrapped 'round the bat's smooth wood. He pressed it down. Right above Eddie's firm hold. "You just witnessed the wear and scare from those shenanigans."

"And you're saying out of town's not?" Eddie removed his hand from the sleek, custom-made bat. Positioned it securely, likewise in fisted wrap-around. Over Dunnigan's. Pressed close

Dunnigan smiled. Kid-on-the-sandlot smile at a summer pickup game. He inserted two open scissor fingers into a V directly onto the bat. Slid them flat above the tight curve of Eddie's grip. "Not saying what questions aren't asked."

~ ~ ~

Over the Hill O' Beans' coffee shop door, the tiny silver bell tinkled once more. Not menacing. Not by any manner. No way, no more. The chipper fellow behind the battered cream-tiled counter looked up. Beamed positive vibes through his winning smile right into how he whistled his happy tune, "Puttin' on the Ritz."

"Hey, there...Mr. Magruder is it?"

"Hey backatcha, son. Eddie Waitkus, it *is*." Magruder hunched below his counter. "Got somethin' here for ya, son." Tossed a folded-over white lunch bag to the wounded baseball player sporting the revitalized gleam.

Waitkus caught the bag open handed. Where it crinkled, it smelled superb. "What's this?"

"Roast beef specialty sandwich, heavy on the Gulden's with a dill. Really no big deal. Nelle hinted heavy you could use some nourishing up before you blew our 'Gansett town."

Surprised as folks can be when a simple, thus strong act of kindness flies at you out of left field, heavy on the Gulden's, Eddie flustered, not quite sure how to volley his return.

"That Nelle, huh? Damn, she's good."

Albert Magruder chuckled. "Yup. That Nelle."

Remembering what and why he'd come back, before backtracking to the train station track, Eddie Waitkus flashed forward one of those lightning strokes of genius which can only be dubbed a *Natural*—in how swell it killed a few birds with one stone—well, in this case—one bat. One bat making one helluva double play. He was doing his lawyer a favor by keeping it out of town, out of harm's way, as he'd been asked. Trouble was, on Wednesday he got word from a weepy secretary that Gerald Dunnigan, Esquire wouldn't be asking any more favors. Dunnigan was dead. Shot in the forehead, dead.

"Well, ain't that somethin'," he countered to the gent behind the counter. "I came back to your mighty fine establishment where I bided my time over the best cup of coffee ever brewed just to give somethin' to your pal, Nelle."

"That so?"

"That's so."

"She help you out of a scrape, Eddie?"

"Uh...could say that." Eddie planted his roast beef specialty safe on the battered counter, sprinted the short distance back to the booth in back that held his backside what seemed days, rather than hours ago. Great. The bat was still there, nestled into seat seams where dark and light green vinyl met each other tight. He hoisted it out. Took a swing. A big league swing. Momentum carried...in the same wide *whoosh* that kindness returning kindness kinda does.

"I *did* say that." Albert Magruder shifted his glass pie dome six inches safer from the edge of the battered cream-tiled counter. "Hey, some bat ya got there, Eddie."

"Yep. Sure is." Eddie felt more than swell. Eddie felt stupendous. Swaggered his bounty to Magruder. Laid the distinguished bat on the battered counter, picked up his meal bag. Grinned large. "That there's for Miss Nelle. She said she was a *solid* baseball fan—not just a regular follower of the greatest sport there is, but she said a *solid* fan. Mr. Magruder, would you kindly give it to her next time she's in? Tell her it's from a grateful first baseman to a *solid* fan. And tell her, would'ya—I'll throw those extra balls she asked for, to those kids in the stands who look like they need a lucky break."

"You got it, bub." Magruder smiled, pausing to run his hand over what seemed like a peculiar looking sweet-spot. He looked up. Reached out. Shook Eddie Waitkus' hand. "Just don't go knockin' on no doors' troubles you don't see comin', hear?"

To his credit, Waitkus laughed. "I promise, Mr. Magruder. Learned my lesson—the hard way." As he tipped the brim of his true blue cap, he was caught by surprise—kindness in the strike zone, once again. Steaming kindness. Eddie caught the white cardboard cup slid his way. Hill O' Beans trademark cup o' joe. Man oh man, this guy thought of everything. "I thank you, sir."

The tiny silver bell tinkled farewell as Eddie Waitkus went out and went on to play deep, to cover as much ground as possible, to be astute enough to make it to first base prior to anything Life threw to a position player. *"Blue skies, nothin' but blue skies"* was the whistle of his happy tune, heard past mere puddles on State Street, that great street.

~ ~ ~

Bell barely got to tinkling when the force of nature that was Nelle Callahan, gusted into the Hill O' Beans.

Rat-a-tat-tat, shot Nelle, right off the bat, "Hi-de-ho! What's it all about, Albie? And hey, my fine friend, I gotta blow! Real soon, with Moe...so...give a nice girl a cup o' joe? To go?"

Tendrils of auburn tresses fluttered faster than her coffee order. Nelle gyrated in thirty-three directions at once, giving one of her fave joints one of her routine lookovers. Thorough. The stuff that *aware,* cascading all corners of the mind at once, is truly made for. She smiled wide at her fave coffee guy, her family friend-to-the-family, who kept an eye on looking out for her best interests. Seemed most of the men of a certain age she knew, did so too. They all claimed they'd loved the mother she'd never got to love. These "designated uncles" knew chapter and verse about her Bootlegger Ma, the beautiful, deceased Angel Tough—but they weren't tellin' no stories. Nosiree. Somethin' was fishy there. More than just for the halibut, they customarily clammed up whenever Nelle got near to the starting gate to interrogate. But come a slew of discerning days, she'd either string up the necklace of their dropped pearls of wisdom, or pummel 'em down and get it out of 'em. She would. Oh yeah, she would.

~ ~ ~

Now wasn't the time though. Nelle had no time. She had to hustle to board the sloop *Angel Courageous* out of Newport. Then sail into New York Harbor during the dark of night with her covert espionage partner. Under convenient cover of his mild national fame as a former Chicago Cubs catcher still touring on global All Star rosters, Moe Berg was a convenient clandestine agent of the new evolving Office of Strategic Services. And Nelle's immediate spy-time handler boss. Her cover as a detective deflected shadows. Provided an unde- tectable means of movement. Who actually knew where a detective on a hot case couldn't cooly go?

After that, the mission ahead got sketchy in the vicinity of how its shadows should, would and could flicker. The dynamic duo had to fly overseas to London. Do some highly classified good stuff for the United States of America. Pull illusions out of his baseball cap, her fedora, or most likely, the standard magician's top hat prop. Illusions call for proper headware y'know. All of this red, white and blue, snappy salute patriotism was served up in only need-to-know dollops for a spy on the sly for Wild Bill Donovan's OSS...which really cut short a gal's day and how she got to shoot the breeze with the folks she hankered for back home. Which reminded—

Lemon Philco up on the high shelf behind the counter played "Something's Gotta Give."

"Say Alb, something's missing around this joint."

"You don't say, Nelle."

"No Albie I *did* just say. Why, that must be where you heard me, Mr Observant. Now, in the immaculate cleanup you did of that crumbum, low-life hood that got in your coffee and doughnut day's way, uh...did you happen to lose sight of a damp fedora with some tall, dark and not so bad on the peepers critter perched underneath it?"

Albert Magruder chuckled. "Took you long enough."

Nelle Callahan countered her counter man. "Did not. I saw what wasn't here on my first spin in.

You know me Alb. I'm the picture of politeness who simply, thus strongly, wishes to chit chat *you* up first." Nelle swiveled another spin, taking more panorama of the Hill O' Beans in. "Priorities be priorities, Albie, and you know you're always Aces high in my closely held hand of grinnin' winners."

Magruder grinned on cue, slid a cup o' joe the way Nelle liked it, heavy on the cream, front and center to where she'd swivel back when she was done posturing her light hearted shenanigans. "Should you be talking about the lemon pie eater, the one who never happily ever ended the tale of the Spoonmaker's Diamond nor the Chocolate Pearl, he —"

"Yes?" Nelle's spin picked up speed. "Ahhh." Nelle's hand picked up coffee.

"Oh, him. He had another piece of pie. He liked it. Really liked it. Bugged me for my recipe for some kindly rooming house lady he knew. But I wouldn't budge. Said the lemon zest particularly reminded him—"

"Albie!"

Magruder's eyes danced to more than what the lemon yellow Philco up on the high shelf began to play as background, *"Some enchanted evening, you may meet a stranger—"*

"Albie! Someday I swear—"

"Now don't swear Nelle. Cursing out what gets under your skin just isn't respectable for a fine lass like you—"

A well-aimed pewter spoon bounced off Magruder's left shoulder.

"Ease up kid. The maybe-Harry man said he'd be back. Said since you couldn't stay in one place too long, he couldn't give you the satisfaction of staying in waiting in that same place too long either, though he really appreciated the extra pieces of pie that got him by. You wanta hear what else he had to say about my lemon pie?"

Nelle sighed. The sigh almost covered the smile Magruder saw sneak out the corner of her pout resistant lips. "Give me the satisfaction," she low-growled. "Like that'll be the day." Torn between missing the opportunity to wing back witty reparteé, yet desperately needing to be on her way, Nelle slapped a buck down on the counter for her nickel cup o' joe and rose from her red swivel stool.

Mid-rise, the bat resting at the back of the battered counter—behind the silver napkin dispenser, the container of striped sippy straws, salt shakers awaiting their refills, plus an array of Heinz tomato ketchup bottles—countered Nelle's roving eye. Intrigued her attention past her departure.

"*Saaay,* Alb. What's that bat doin' here? You beating down the competition?"

Albert Magruder shook his head, plenty used to Nelle's quicksilver jive. He took it in good-naturedly, same way he admired her style. Nelle's style was like the insight and curiosity of six lucky cats on a porch full of rockers that one knew to keep careful around. He'd solemnly promised his favorite nephew, Doc Nelson, same as he'd vowed to Doc's sweet, loving partner, Angel Towse Callahan—the *Charm and Courage Bootlegger*—that he'd be vigilant concerning their gal's safety and not let anything slip out to reveal her future... until the time was right. That was near twenty years ago. Time wasn't right yet.

"It's a bat, Nelle."

"I can *see* that, Albie. What? You think I'm blind as a—"

"Funny girl—Fanny Brice has got nuttin' on you, kid. Eddie left it. Left it special for you when he left with his roast beef special. He said to tell you—"

~ ~ ~

It wasn't cool breezin' that blew the next tinkle over the door of the Hill O' Beans. It was a cliché. Tall, dark and handsome blew straight in. The evasive prospective client who wanted to be taken seriously, yet wished to be secretively undivulged. Just a plain old Harry. Nelle fathomed without even going deep, there was nothing plain about this Harry, no matter what his name turned out to be. She also knew, unfortunately, she had no time at the time to fathom the big lug further—who he was, where his case could lead, what his attraction held. *Oh brother, the bother of loose ends.*

"Well *there* she is," the non-Harry type hyped. "Dazzling detective dame returning to the scene of the story of the crime she ran away from—"

The rise he roused was low-level. But that was the rub. Nelle stepped up to rub his rouse back, poked one ruby fingernail into the soggy shoulder seam of his still soggy trench. Taunted back, "Hey, bub, I'll have you know I run away from *no* trouble. And—you? Why, I deduce you're...*big*... Trouble. Capital *T* kinda trouble. Yep. That's what *you* be. Capital T."

"Ahhh, so the lady has a good sense of spell," the man not Harry smirked, settling onto the swivel stool nearest his nonchalance. "But can you sit a spell, Nelle? Go over the terms of how you're going to go over my case?" He patted the next stool. Quirked a brow. His left.

Which left her damned to make this right. With time way too damn tight.

More razzed than jazzed, Nelle spouted, "Why you...*you*...you non-Harry gadabout who lost a will and lost a chocolate pearl bequest and lost the story threads Albie spun best to teeter a tale about a Turkish Spoonmaker's Diamond—"

"Get to the point to make your point, Callahan."

Lemon Philco up on the high shelf behind the battered counter wafted strains of Ella Fitzgerald. "Someone To Watch Over Me." Magruder looked up. Nodded soft and sweet, as he recognized, reverently—the no-such-thing-as-a-coincidence hallmark of how Angel Tough lived life. Fully. Past mere earthly boundaries. Philco shifted to "Don't Fence Me In." Oh, that Angel, she could make her mark on a scene, even through a little lemon yellow music machine. He stood straighter. Took over his watch. *I got this covered honey,* he whispered inside his head. Funny, in a warm way, he felt her immediate response, felt temperatures rising—in gradual degrees as Angel's hot smile and wise counsel never failed to stir the air around mere reality.

Albert interrupted the spit of the counter couple's spat. Picked up the spectacular bat.

Now that got attentions focused. Center field of vision, in nothin' flat.

"Hey, *great* bat!" not-Harry exclaimed. "May I?" His reach was pure, sure grab.

"Hey, you! That's *my* bat."

"Yours? You got *another* career I don't know about under the flirty, flirty angle of how you flaunt your own fedora, which is rather soft and dry by the way. How do you do that?"

"My fedora's got nuttin' flirty flickin' its brim *your* way, hotshot. Now gimme my bat!" Nelle's moxie, sparked when provoked, propelled at one speed and one speed only. Speed o' light. Her reach lunged to eclipse his grab. Jostled jib over his jab, "And my career moves are *nobody's* shimmies but my own. Hey, why's it any of your business, anyway, big guy?"

Non-Harry's grasp of the situation, as well as the spectacular bat, deftly maneuvered the prize away, clean out of Nelle's lunge reach. He took firm hold at the taper. Pulled the barrel back.

Nelle hesitated. Saw Albie hustling cream colored mugs and cobalt saucers clear...to the furthest safe end of the counter. While he was at it, he stayed right there.

"Maybe..." Non-Harry swung out. Sliced into one crisp *whooooosh*. "Maybe I have a vested interest in your business, Callahan." Ignoring Nelle's eyebrows elevating exclamatory danger marks, he stated, within his arc of authority—which was syncing a wide swing—and to the level best of his concentration, "Why, this baby must be a *Deluxe Burley*, an A.J. Reach special. Hmm. The weight's over forty-ounces. The length is pushing past thirty-four. Plus this distinct tint—"

"Hey, yourself. Hold up there, slugger! How'd you go figure your figurings fast as your first swing?

The man with the bat paused. Poised his pause along with the spectacular bat. Vertically. Upright on the checkered linoleum before the lady's fashionably shod feet. Faux-Harry hunched forward with both hands gripping the smooth knob. "Well, I've been a kid in my life, Callahan. Kids play ball. They remember stuff." He shot a seductive grin into her calculating peepers. Shifted her train of thought with his trajectory. Then blindsided a quick jab to her aplomb. "So...*great!* You're taking my case. Let's get started, Nelle. Now."

"You *stating* or requesting?" Nelle deflected the feeble attempt at her aplomb. Nobody messed with Nelle's aplomb. Matter o' fact, world needed more aplomb.

"It's obvious. You're taking my case."

"Obvious, huh?"

"Sure, a guy hangs around your quick getaway scenes long enough he deduces that your rebuff and return means you'll come back. You came back this time for loose ends you don't like to leave tangled." He took in her scowl. Made no effort to hide his returning grin. "Hah! I nailed you Nelle, didn't I?"

No one upper-handed Nelle, especially with her own lines. Time to up the ante of this deal. "Okay then, smartypants. Settle up my fee?"

"Shoot."

"Careful when you say that around Nelle," came Magruder's voice, still safe, snug and secure midst saucers and smirks at the better end of his battered counter.

Nelle bit in her grin. Raised and waggled three fingers. "Okay then. First third? My retainer up front. Second third comes due at your reveal. Final third to be paid in full upon wrap-up of all non-tanglings. Fair enough?"

"Tough call, lady." He threw her for a loop with an answer outta left field.

She recovered. Pronto. Nelle nibbled no bait. "What? You *afraid* of tough calls?"

His hesitation? Brief, though long enough to contemplate repercussions. Without looking side-ways, he felt Albert's eyes. Honed on his response, like the guy knew how he was going to field and pepper this one. "Actually, Callahan, in *my* line of work I come across tough calls all the time. Sometimes tough calls are bad calls. Sometimes they cost me what I came there to do."

Nelle didn't skip a beat. Inside though, she played his striking words over—once, twice, three times. "If you don't know your name, but you know your line of work, what *is it* you do?"

The not hurried not-Harry respectfully returned the bat to the battered counter. Rounded his return to Nelle with palms wide open. Cool gaze likewise. Cool gaze saw warm assessment. Something told him he liked that. Something told him not to let this quick cookie know, right off the bat, what he liked, what he didn't like. Best keep his verbal vibes under vigilant radar. "Let's just say...I start my day on an even playing field."

"Even playing field, huh?"

He shifted her deducing. Best defense is offense. "Can you say the same, Callahan?"

Nelle paused. Affirmed where she was going—which was further. "Truth?"

"Truth."

"Well then, damp fedora fella, *whatever* your name turns out to be, for me, the *truth* is, some days the deck is stacked against me before I can even say *Hocus Focus* and discern where a joker's hiding, and where the aces ain't."

"Ahh, gambler, magician, sleuth—any other occupational habits up your trench sleeve?"

"Can't say."

"Can't say or won't say?" he taunted.

Nelle thought fast.

Not-Harry assessed...slow. Thorough.

"Listen, Harry—which is not your real name come hell or high water—"

"You ever see me in hell or high water?" He was enjoying this.

"Don't divert."

"Divert the amazing Nelle Callahan? Nah. Never happen—come hell or high water, come rain or come shine."

Amused, Nelle eased one slender hip onto the edge of one red swivel stool. One elbow pressed against the battered counter, aware of pressing time, wary of a worthy adversary. Still, Nelle was flying all sails full speed ahead. New horizons are always worth their discovery.

Unused to soft silence, smiling silence, as a bonafide response to how Callahan usually scuttled her comeback patter, make-believe Harry threw a quick changeup, "You didn't name your retainer." He reached inside his trench. Pulled and flipped opened his wallet. "What do I owe for your first-third down?"

"Your name."

"Beg your pardon?"

"A grown man of substance shouldn't go begging, Mr. What's-Your-Name."

Magruder's cups and saucers end of the counter dished out a chuckle. Then a chortle.

Slightly flustered, the fellow 'neath the damp fedora pivoted his once sure footing. "Ah, let's go back a step. I inquired what was your first third—"

"And I responded, *What's your name?*"

"*What's your name?* is your first-third?"

"No, who's on first, which is me, short of time by the way, and let's not Abbot and Costello this around." She glared. Convincingly.

He took off his fedora. Likewise his glib demeanor. His hand reached for hers. "Alright, Callahan. You can call me Katch."

She accepted his substantially warm paw. Warmly. Shook it. "Catch?"

"Katch."

"Like catch-me-if-you-can? Catch-a-falling-star-and-put-it-in-your-pocket?"

He kept hold of her hand. More warmly. More substantial. "We'll see."

"Catch, if there's one thing I hate, it's the shortsighted phrase *We'll see*," Nelle griped, tugging loose her hand. "Leaves all kinds of loose ends."

He chuckled. So did Magruder's end of the counter. "Speaking of loose ends—"

Nelle slid off her swivel stool and left it swiveling. Jangled three fingers in his face, one at a time, closer than before. "You want me to find the will your dead lawyer is no longer alive enough to have in his possession. You want me to track down this Chocolate Pearl that means more than a family fortune to you. And...you want me to believe these loose ends tie into Albie's half-served story of the Spoonmaker's Diamond in Istanbul, which is not Constantinople by the way. Sure seems I've got all your bases covered."

A *guffaw* from the Magruder end of the counter this time.

Katch kept counsel. His turn to dole the silent treatment, wait out her next pitch.

Nelle, pressed for time she no longer had time to press on with, crafted decision to solution. Challenged his shoulder chip to rouse the rise she expected. "So, I'm taking your case, *after*—"

"*After!*" He cut her off like a runner with a long lead at first. "After?"

Nelle whirled. Blew a kiss, dashed a jaunty wave at the safe cup-and-saucer-keeper down the battered counter. Hollered with gusto, "See ya, Albie!" Then turned. Radiated smile, extended her right hand. Back to where she'd just felt warmth. Substantial warmth. Softer than her average holler she soft-hollered, "See you, Catch. After I complete a commitment I'm committed to. But I'll be back. Tell you what. Why don't you keep my bat as collateral? See, how's that? Ya see, I *like* that bat. I'd never let you keep that bat, my bat. That bat came to me by way of a big league ballplayer and I'm one of the most *solid* fans of our national pastime, so trust me, Mr. Catch, I'll be back for that bat. No doubt about it. Case open to be case closed." She smiled. Waited.

He accepted her hand. Likewise her smile. Felt her recurring warmth. Substantially. Held all of that once more, past the mere shaking part of agreement between parties to agree.

She winked. "So no loose ends to Catch."

~ ~ ~

The Hill O' Beans' bell tinkled and the room no longer did.

Both men felt the presence of her absence.

Magruder shoved gloom from the room in the most effective way he knew. Logically. Plunked a pot of the finest brew any evening got more robust with, next to the bat on his battered counter. Looked the other guy in the eye as men who are on to each other are prone to do. "Knew I knew your look from somewhere in my time. Tell you what. There's another piece of pie on the house if you'll stick around, Mister. Tell me the answer to my next question."

"Lemon?"

"Yup."

"Never knew I'd find the kind of lemon pie I'd never pass up," Katch answered glibly.

Magruder though—all business. "I saw you in the bullpen with Dizzy Dean. Didn't I?"

Coffee, pie or countering a real good counter guy—one or all of the three shook off the man's guarded mood. Likewise his trench. He wound up. Slyly dodged and sidearmed his response, "You know what the docs found when they x-rayed Dizzy Dean's head?"

"NOTHING!" both men exploded in the simultaneous chorus which begins a fine friendship.

The younger stuck out his hand, "Paul Katchernick. Real pleased to know you, Mr. Magruder. They Americanized my name to Katcher—*To make it fit*, they said, when Topps printed out my first rookie run of baseball cards."

"Call me Albie. And imagine that," he said,

edging the bat out of striking range of two hot coffees on the pour, "as I live and breathe, I've got a pitcher named Katcher at my counter."

Katcher grinned, reached one hand for the fork placed at the side of the lemon pie he was growing fonder than fonder of. Idly, several fingers from his other hand pressed in the edge of the shiny black tape that had loosened near the knob on the pale green tinted bat.

Albie watched the Chicago Cubs rookie. Thought gently about why his problems in this world amounted to something at the Hill O' Beans. "Some bat, huh?" he said softly.

The pitcher, Katcher, tightened the black tape, looping it back round the bat's slender neck, while savoring mouthfuls of exquisite lemon pie. He admired the bat more at each loop. At each meticulous inspection. "It's called the *Green Wonder*. There were only a few made by the A.J. Reach Sporting Goods Company. A.J. started out in Philly, you know. Figured there was enough to this game called baseball that it would be a good business to make it his business to supply bats, balls and other sporting equipment. The great ballplayer, Connie Mack, hooked up with him and took a long look at his growing business. Winning combination. Those guys hit off a profitable success with the major leagues, then the college leagues, and finally thousands of exuberant youth leagues. They adjusted their bats in stature and weight to fit the occasion of the precise game about to be played."

"You seem to know a lot about the Reach bats."

"My pop taught me. Taught me good." Paul Katcher reached enthusiastically for his fork again, but stopped, frustrated, as the loose black tape wasn't staying stuck. "Matter of fact—"

~ ~ ~

A guy goes silent is one small thing. A guy quits eating his lemon pie is a big another. Magruder looked concern at the guy's concern. "Hey, alright there, Katcher?"

Guy was stone cold quiet. Pie was getting more untouched.

Magruder tried again, "You said *Matter o' fact.* Matter o' fact what? What's eatin' you that you're not eatin', fella?"

The shiny black tape loosened at his quick tug. A long strand of it pulled off. Left behind a blotched white stickiness over the revealed wood. Paul Katcher pulled more, stretched further. The tape unraveled. Peeled and pulled off. "Holy cow, Mr. Magruder, this is *my dad's* bat!"

"Nope. No way. I know the guy who brung it in."

"Who?"

"Eddie Waitkus. Plays for—"

"Philly!" chorused the two men countering one friendship to one going further.

"Philadelphia is where my father's from, where my family's from—where I just came from—the funeral from—from where I found my father's lawyer, not in possession of—"

Albie sustained a steady hand, as well as a steady eye on the guy. Topped off his porcelain mug with the best cup o' joe that could break the spell of too much percolating drama. "Lot of coincidences you've got spinning your imagination, Katcher. It *couldn't* be—"

"Oh, but it *is*. See there? See, Mr. Magruder, I mean, Albie, see those marks? This bat was my best present on my eighth birthday. Pop said he'd teach me more and more about baseball every year and then, come every birthday, I'd be better. He said a great bat would make a great player a *champ*. He cautioned though, that I always take super good care of *this* bat. Explained how he knew A.J. How Mr. Reach would design a single bat style each year that was not the norm. That way, he never let his winning business diminish to a slump. Like a batting average taking a dive in July, he never wished that kind of slump on profits and probabilities. So there were only *three* of the pale green White Northern Ashes crafted that year. *1931. White Northern Ash hits the strongest, goes the longest,* Pop told me. He said A.J. Reach told him, *This bat would work wonders, I'd see...when the time was right.* And then—"

"Then, what? And *what* markings are you talking about?"

"He took it away. Dad was mad. Said I wouldn't see it again 'til I appreciated its power."

"Wait. Why'd he take it away? What the hell'd you do, Katcher?"

Dispirited, the man no longer delighting in the merits of lemon pie looked down and downcast at the battered counter. Fingering the bat, remembering, he scuffed at particles of stubborn white residue with his fingernail. "It was my second best gift that got me in trouble."

"I don't follow."

"Pen knife. But I got tired of just playing mumbletypeg in the yard with my buddies. I snuck us in to Dad's den. Wanted to show off. So I showed off and showed them my bat. Told them his stories. They dared me. I caved. Pulled out my new pen knife. Carved in my new name."

Albie scrutinized curvy lines upside down from the other side of the bat. "I don't see no '*K*' nowhere. You didn't carve in *Katchernick?*"

Sheepishly, Paul looked up. Answered straight about those curves. "*C-H-A-M-P*...Albie, those were the letters I carved right into this bat and that was that. My old man took it away. Said he'd teach me the difference between respect and child's play. I was eight, Albie. I learned a life lesson—that young, the hard way."

Magruder shook his head. "Seems I'm hearing that line a lot around here today." He hesitated. Considered Katch's story, then speculated kindly, "Shame though—"

"Shame? Shame about what?"

"Well, Paul, I'm deeply sorry about the recent loss of your father. He sounds to me like a guy who loved his kid. A lot. Shame he didn't get to give you back your bat when you'd *appreciate its power*, like he said. Surely he went to your games? Saw how swell you were makin' it up the Big Leagues?"

"Every game he could, Albie. That amounted to a lot of games. He had reasons and means to travel. And he did. Surprised me many times, just showing up at the team's hotel. Took me out for a T-bone, mashed potatoes and green beans dinner."

"I don't get it. Then... *why?*"

With most of the white adhesive scraped from the tinted green wood under the slick black tape, Paul Katcher lovingly stroked his memories along with the unsticky length of the previously concealed sweet spot of his bat—well, technically, Nelle's bat. But he'd handle that. Back and forth, forth and back. He glanced up, ready to respond best way he could to Magruder, and his finger caught a rough bump in the smooth. No, two rough bumps in the smooth. Two miniscule brass brads, securing a clasp to release...

"Holy mackerel, Andy!" Magruder yelped when Katcher released a catch. A small-scale catch. So small, so puny that, up until this moment in time, had not been noticeable in keeping the neck and knob intact on this stunning, distinctively tinted *Green Wonder* bat.

"Christopher Columbus, will you look at that!"

Katcher twisted the knob a quarter turn. It opened to a lead-weighted hollow tube.

Thing was, the tube wasn't absolutely hollow. Albie realized he heard a version of Nelle's favorite refrain inside his head, *Sometimes illusions aren't what they're cracked up to be.* What he didn't realize was that he'd repeated her words out loud.

Katcher did. A humdinger of a look crossed his

face. He shook the tinted White Northern Ash *Green Wonder*. The *illusion* of *stronger and longer* sure made a helluva lot more sense now. Now that he was older than eight. Now that he understood why he'd had to wait. A sheaf of scrolled parchment glided out. Slid silently to the battered counter.

Albie moved away the coffee. *Expeditiously.*

The power of the bat was finally appreciated. *Exponentially.*

In attuned chorus, new friends read aloud old words sprawled before them.

The Last Will and Testament
of Michael Matthew Katchernick

Pitcher Paul Katcher struck out the stunned silence at the Hill O' Beans with a hushed, slow-breaking fadeaway, "That Nelle. Damn. She's *good.*"

Wise Albert Magruder bobbed his head. Grinned. "Yup. That Nelle."

Narragansett Times

Saturday, August 18, 1944
Waitkus Waits No More!

MLB Commissioner Happy Chandler is more than happy to announce the return of first baseman Eddie Waitkus to rightful stance and stature for the Philadelphia Phillies.

Waitkus, victim of a bizarre rifle shooting at a Chicago away game, in the Edgewater Beach Hotel, by crazed-in-love fan Ruth Ann Steinhagen, was declared, "Fully recovered with vim and vigor!" by Dr. I.B. Leeve, following rigorous workouts by team trainer Wally Maggda.

Reached for comment, Waitkus waved high his navy Phillies cap and said, "No funny business for that honey, no more."

L.A. sources credit Narragansett Detective Nelle Callahan's tip linking 19-year-old Steinhagen to movie star Alan Ladd and Cubs Peanut Lowrey stalkings. Evidence of hit list shrines and Boston baked beans pyramid stacks in her N. Chicago apartment confirmed findings.

Charged with assault with intent to murder, Steinhagen was declared insane and committed to psychiatric care. Season tickets for '45 Cubs remain at large.

~ ~ ~

Overheard at sea, aboard the *ANGEL COURA-GEOUS*, somewhere between Beaver Tail Lighthouse on Conanicut Island, rounding the Point Judith lighthouse.

Moe: "So, you got to the Commish?"

Nelle: "Yep. How's Eddie now?"

Moe: "Crazy-happy. Whatcha think? So how'd you pull it off? I mean, with Happy Chandler? Did you need to use our boss man?"

Nelle: "Wild Bill Donovan?"

Moe: "The OSS's one and only."

Nelle: "Not quite."

Moe: "What d'ya mean, kid?"

Nelle: "Illusions aren't always what you think they are."

Moe: "Espionage Etiquette 101. That's on the beam, Nelle. But you're tryin' to tell me a man's name is *not* a man's name when he's the most powerful undercover chief of the Operation of Strategic Services in the U.S. of A.?

Nelle: "Nope. Means sometimes there's two names that make the same difference."

Moe: "Never thought I'd say this, Nelle, since you're supposed to be learning the finer points of this spy business from my seasoned expertise, but back in my baseball career, I know when something's coming in from leftfield. *You?* I don't catch your drift. I'm losing ya, kid."

Nelle, punching her partner's arm; snicker-inclusive: "Big league catcher like you, Moe Berg? *Hah!* You're hardly worth your secret identity cover for the safety and protection of our country, are ya then? And, Moe, you big lug, you'll never lose me. You've got vision where the rest of the world wears bifocals."

Moe, rubbing his arm; eye-rolling inclusive: "That's a swell line, Nelle."

Nelle: "Think I should write it down?"

Moe: "Nah. Your whipper-snapper of a photographic mind will remember it. Probably pawn it off on some up-and-comer author. Then the guy'll make screen gems millions with it."

Nelle: "As long as he doesn't use too much dynamite with it, he can sundance his way to it, butch."

Moe: "C'mon there, banter queen. Tell me how Wild Bill Donovan's *name* twisted the arm of Baseball Commissioner Happy Chandler's decision to get Eddie Waitkus reinstated faster than a seventh-inning stretch."

Nelle: "Easy peasy, chucklehead. Took no floy floy. I done some diggin' *plus* it's what I always tell you."

Moe: "So you're tellin' me now, it took no nonsense to get the job done, huh. But what? You tell me a lot of things. Boy oh boy, man oh man, every day we're on a case, Nelle, all you do is talk, talk, talk—tell, tell, tell—"

Nelle punches his arm again. Harder; without the snicker this time.

Moe: "Sorry, partner. G'head."

Nelle: "Well you see, it just so turns out Happy Chandler had a best buddy back in Detroit."

Moe: "Lot of people have best buddies."

Nelle: "This one had a nickname."

Moe: "Lotta best buddies come with nicknames attached. Makes them handy. Distinctive."

Nelle: "His sure was. *Wild Bill Donovan.*"

Moe: "No shit. No way. A baseball player? And no relation to *our* Wild Bill?"

Nelle: "No shit, Dick Tracy. *Tigers.* No relation. He's a much older chap now. So I told Happy Chandler—"

Moe: "That he'd be happy to hear—"

Nelle, grinning: "That there's no such thing as a coincidence."

Moe: "Sheesh, you're a pistol, Nelle."

Nelle patted her pocket, showing her partner she was serious about the business of their business. A good Narragansett breeze loosened and untangled auburn tresses to fly free. Brisk. Brash. Unfettered. Like the mood of the moment. Her attention shift-

ed, reflexively to the What's Next of any situation she found herself in. "So? Moe? Where we off to after New York and London?"

Moe: "Istanbul."

Nelle: "It's not Constantinople."

Moe: "Knew you were gonna say that."

STAY TUNED...

There'll be more.

There's always more brewing than a Hill O' Beans' when international Trouble's on the scene.

~ ~ ~

I'm Detective Nelle Callahan.

I've met some of you before and no doubt I'll run a look-over on some of you when we meet up on some dark rendezvous that spooks or sparks a soul. But for now, I DO gotta case with a dead guy and something to find, as well as finding out why I should be finding it for a fellow who finally told a dame his name. And I'm on a secret mission, which means I can't talk to you about that. I'll keep you posted though. You take care now. Don't take any wooden nickels, hear?

HISTORICAL NOTES TO *NOTE*

In the oft said, *"You can't make stuff like this up"* realm, the Nelle Callahan noirvella serial tales of suspense and intrigue are laced and interwoven with threads of 1920s to 1940s history, complete with colorful characters prominent to the eras.

Truer Than Fine Fiction

WILD BILL DONOVAN and the OSS (Office of Strategic Services)

General William Donovan was hand-picked by the Columbia law school upper-classman who became President Franklin Delano Roosevelt—to fill the glaring espionage and intelligence gathering gap the United States of America suffered in the pre-war 1940s. America's chief spy-master was given a generous hand across the sea by the British SIS— Secret Intelligence Service. That Churchill fellow and Donovan's spy bloke counterpart, Stewart Menzies, made history the real deal in Donovan dealings. The OSS became the U.S.A.'s CIA

(Central Intelligence Agency, under department heads originally trained in spycraft by their beloved chief, Wild Bill). The SIS evolved to today's MI-6 (Military Intelligence, section 6). Though rumored that agent Nelle Callahan taught a young lad named Jimmy Bond a thing or three, this author cannot or will not precisely confirm. *Some illusions are best left illusions.*

MOE BERG, MLB catcher and OSS spy

Knight-errant Morris Berg was the genuine stuff of chivalry, a finger to the mouth *"Shh"*-sayer for questions preferred unanswered, and the most knowledgeable man in major league baseball from 1926 to 1939. He graduated from Princeton, studied law, spoke twelve languages fluently, and consumed all facets of knowledge. Moe was serious, light-hearted, and the ballplayer whom eccentric Casey Stengel called "the strangest man ever to play baseball." His masterful mind recalled batters' habits, quirks and tells, making him one of the best defensive catchers for the Cleveland Indians, Boston Red Sox, Washington Senators and Chicago White Sox.

Baseball access to international All-Star team travels, a masterful mind of the times and Moe's mysterious manner of appearing and vanishing, gave him baseline plus superstar skills for the OSS recruitment which led to missions in South America, Japan, Yugoslavia, Czechoslovkia and more, much more...especially when paired off with the devlish moxie of agent Nelle Callahan. Marvel at Moe's WWII espionage exploits in *Magic Spy*, the second release in my noirvella series, as well as *Say It Ain't So, Moe.* That's all Moe and Nelle wanted me to verify right now. They're on a mission. *"Shhhh."*

The BOOTLEGGING business of Narragansett Bay, Rhode Island

America's thirst during Prohibition was quenched by the watery rum runners of the Ocean State. Swift Rhode Island cigarette boats, built twelve to every one ordered from the exact plans the Coast Guard commissioned local shipbuilders, skimmed cross currents as a shore thing. Crime bosses Bugsy Siegel, Meyer Lansky, that nasty Joey Adonis, Arnie Rothstein, Waxey Gordon, Big Bill Dwyer, Owney Madden and some fella known as Joe Kennedy cornered the Canadian cash markets of the spirited Bronfman brothers. Harry and Sam's Seagram poured from Nova Scotia to Boston to New York, lapping lucrative along Long Island into Narragansett Bay up Newport way. America's speak-

easies spoke loud and clear for what Nelle Callahan's mother, the "Charm and Courage Bootlegger," procured. Devotion to the daring lady pro-
viding Depression-era jobs for farmers with beat up
trucks, former dandies with idle Model T's and
fishermen switching bait for more than just the
halibut flowed like success hauled into tunnels on
moonlit nights. But that's another noirvella story,
Angel Tough, the Charm and Courage Bootlegger,
for another thoughtful reading time.

**EDDIE WAITKUS, first baseman for the
Philadelphia Phillies, shot at Chicago's Edgewater Hotel by deranged stalker RUTH ANN
STEINHAGEN, who likewise put fear of fame
into movie star Alan Ladd and Chicago Cubs
baseball ace, Peanut Lowrey**

Eddie Waitkus played first for the Cubs and then
the Phillies and sure should have stayed in his own
hotel room after a certain away game back at Wrig-
ley Field. He was a fine defensive first baseman, a
solid line-drive hitter. Even made the All-Star team.
Real nice guy, not at all a horndog. Eddie didn't
deserve the unlucky shot he got. To the chest.
Though I've adjusted the date by a few years to
keep time with Nelle and Moe's next mission to
London whisking Winston Churchill's wishes, the

sad-sack story Eddie lamented to Nelle and his injury time out of America's greatest pastime is all detailed, tragic and true. True too is Ruth Ann's weird stalking fame fetish.

Extensive 1940s take-me-out-to-the-ballgame research intrigued me to give Eddie a wide playing field to jaw his genuine beef. I didn't correlate, 'til after this tale was told, that a handsome fella named Robert Redford became Roy Hobbs in *The Natural* movie version of crazed Ruth Ann's rifle shot heard 'round the Edgewater. Writer Bernard Malamud fictionalized what Barry Levinson hit "outta da park" as iconic baseball movies go, but I gave you folks the facts, nuttin' but the facts. Baseball Commissioner Happy Chandler was making his decisions stick like pine tar back then, and actually had a coincidence pal—convenient for Nelle—likewise named Bill Donovan. Oh, that Nelle. She can talk her way in and outta any fix. Bold as a comeback batting average.

The green-tinted A.J. Reach Deluxe Burley wonder bat

Indeed, it's all it's not cracked up to be. Legend assures that the solid White Northern Ash hits the strongest, projects the longest, swings wide and free. Philadelphia Phillies franchise founder and first open contract baseball player, London born Alfred James Reach, opened the A.J. Reach Company as a popular Philly athletic goods store in 1874, when he put down his leather glove. Success smacked like homers and Reach built a factory to perceptively produce sporting equipment. Designed a single bat style each year that stood out from the norm. There were only three of the pale green White Northern Ashes crafted in the year 1931, and, as my noirvella tells, a well-off gent by the name of Michael Matthew Katchernick purchased one. For his son. For the love of baseball. For what sports history would become for a pitcher dubbed Katcher. Ahhh, another solid hit tale for another super reading time. You'll see in *The Magic Spy* as well as *It's Noir or Never.*

The A.J. Reach Company, with dedication to excellence and clever, entrepreneurial advertising to youth leagues, college leagues and major leagues, became the largest manufacturer of sporting goods in the United States during the 19th and 20th centuries. Spalding and Brothers paid handsomely to buy the company...and the reach of Reach.

McGillin's Olde Ale House, serving McGillin's renowned Genuine Lager

Philadelphia's finest, I assure you. Opened as the Bell In Hand Tavern by "Ma" and "Pa" McGillin as laboring locals hailed them. Notoriety poured and nickname stuck like wet bar rings on an oak bar...from the year Lincoln was toasted by tavern mugs raised high. McGillin's taps flowed on after the Liberty Bell was all it was cracked up to be, outlasted the Civil War and kept its head past Prohibition, assuring its place in history—Philadelphia's oldest continuously operating tavern, thus one of the most renowned Irish pubs in the United States of America.

When Pa died, Ma McGillin carried on, keeping a list of troublemakers she wouldn't let in. List read like the social register in Philly, always a boon for brewing business. Named consecutive years to "Top 100 U. S. Nightclubs and Bars", McGillin's has been a big hit with sports fans, Vaudeville to show-biz folks, naturally politicos and hobnobbers. Where else would an attorney of the stature of Gerald Dunnigan, Esquire be sought and found by on-the-ball Eddie Waitkus?

McGillin's own brewed beer is unfiltered, as it

would've been in the 1800s. The secret recipe of multiple hop varieties could not be cracked by Moe Berg, when Eddie bought a fellow ballplayer a cool one on a hot Philly afternoon. Moe did detect centennial and amarillo in the blend though, and Ma concurred. Told ya. That Moe Berg's a smart one. Moe's mighty mind moves more than mountains, when Nelle sparks her signature blend—spycraft magic. McGillin's, located conveniently on a tiny alley running behind Philadelphia City Hall, welcomes all-stars again when the Democratic National Convention comes to town, offering "The Dublin Donkey" (ginger beer with a shot of Jameson). *Listen.* Is that Hillary or one of those Kennedy boys returning to karoke for their beer?

The tunes which play no such thing as a coincidence accompaniment, from the lemon-yellow Philco, high on a shelf at The Hill O' Beans?

Indeed, Glenn Miller assured Nelle Callahan that they all made The Hit Parade in America. Dial in to 1940 on your own handy transistor, MP3 player, Spotify or headphone hookups. They'll still carry you past time and time again...and leave their mental message. *Somewhere there's music. How faint the tune.* Bing Crosby and Ella Fitzgerald just ordered another slice of lemon pie to go with their cups o' joe and concurred. I believe I heard them. Did you?

The HILL O' BEANS Coffee Shop

Gosh darn it. Sure wish that spiffy place was real and that I could meet you there, treasured reader. We'd select a swivel stool and have the best cup o' joe any rainy night could brew. I'd pick up the tab. We might even consider the lemon pie.

~ *Author Kate Pilarcik,* who absolutely believes in detective/OSS agent Nelle Callahan's daring do, and is quite pleased parts of your higher mind does now too. There come times when illusions truly *can* be all they're cracked up to be. You'll see. Yeah, you'll see. In the next intrigue epic-sode of my noirvella series, *Magic Spy,* OSS espionage agents Nelle Callahan and Moe Berg, with SIS cunning counterparts, make a veritable difference in how the world as we know it was altered through behind the scenes WWII tenacious tactics. Much more than tricks pulled out of a black silk hat or sleight of hand handed down by Harry Houdini's protégé, magician John Muholland, armed the OSS in spytime subterfuge. Muholland prepped and propped this dynamic duo, during the time he was hired to write the first U.S. spycraft manual. Chapters changed in how history paged out. Volumes.

Grace of my Thanks for your reading and following mine and Nelle's intrigue trail.

We can promise you only... "never a dull moment", but that's what keeps illusions fresh, eh?

ACKNOWLEDGMENTS

There come killer-diller sparks when Nelle Callahan whispers me her tales of intrigue. That's 1940's slang, or *"good stuff!"* as Nelle wisecracks, keeping time with her Juicy Fruit gum. Shadows virtually shimmy. My keyboard klickety-klacks, klackety-klicks, transcending time and time again, as moxie takes on mayhem. World needs more moxie. You darn well know it does.

So I thank Nelle and the swell chums she blends into our genuine scenes of cultural and political history while tunes of their era play. There's a lot to be said for era and atmosphere...getting lost in it, only to be found the more. I thank the Dorsey Brothers, Benny Goodman, Harry James and Glenn Miller for jazz-intoned instrumentals and ballads backing my crooners. Miss Billie Holliday, Ella Fitzgerald, Evelyn Knight, Edith Piaf, Jo Stafford, Julie London, Nat King Cole, Bing Crosby, Charlie Parker, Artie Shaw and a lanky Sinatra boy named Frankie—I could not have written back in time without you.

Illusions exist with Nelle, yet no-such-thing-as-a-coincidence. I believe I was led to live, love, write and promote from the very bootlegger-era home Nelle Callahan would've grown up in. From tiny Vienna, Ohio roots and family-based Bristol, Connecticut years, I now wake in Wakefield, nestled next to Narragansett Bay, in big-hearted little Rhode Island. Within a 1925 humdinger of an American Four Square. You'll read about it in *Angel Touch, the Charm and Courage Bootlegger*, along the noirvella trail of intrigue you've stepped into and up to. Grace o' my thanks to the fine tuning (and refined tuning) of editor-in-chief and noirtorious publisher Eric Campbell and Down & Out Books. Our quantum "team" approach of noir-thriller-crime writers stir and spur us. Further. Farther. Our Jason Smith surpasses book cover artist and illustrator status. He's the visual impressionist of protagonists come alive. Soft thanks, good sir.

The stuff of soul-stir and psyche-spark reinforces for this publishing-promoter-author, that we offer our readers more in our own writing spanse by influences we take in and give back from our community of fellow scribes. Nelle's first vocal friends were authors on their soar, encouraging to write, and write more—Harry B. Sanderford, Kevin Michaels, the late and ever great A.J. Hayes, and my gobsmacking Brits, Col Bury, Matt Hilton and lovely Bohemian sister Lily Childs. You all know where you generate gusto.

There. You know of me, my publishing house

and Nelle, Moe, watchful Albie and a pitcher named Katcher. Plenty more memorable characters are coming along history's way. But let us know some about you too, will'ya? The kinds of reads which move you. When you laugh out loud, roll your eyes or go one more page, and then another, getting lost to be found again. *That's reading.* That's what Nelle and I and Down & Out Books wish to give you with our intrigue serial of noir-vellas. Find us where reviews are writ and social media sparks.

Couldn't close an acknowledgement without my heart thoroughly thanking (best way a heart thanks) "Prof," historian, educator and wise world citizen Matthew Magda, who claimed my writing flowed like water and never let up urging the splash, while making sure my Roosevelt years were in sync with how Nelle's tales said they were in sync. I listened. Grew to love the guy. Gonna marry him at sea next year. Funny how life travels when you soar only towards the best. Speaking of which, brother Dave, Navy Captain pal Sharon, son Josh and daughter Julie read and questioned and kept me grounded on Nelle's exploits, while son-in-law Officer Mike shares generous his vast knowledge of police lore. My hero, my dad, Paul Pilarcik, taught,

ACKNOWLEDGMENTS

"It's the folks who matter who provide our true enrichment."

Like you. Nelle and I thank you all...readers, influencers and those around life's next bend.

~ Kate Pilarcik, absolutely
~ Wakefield, Rhode Island, circa 2016

KATE PILARCIK, suspense author and intrigue promoter (as Absolutely*Kate), has moxie. World needs more moxie. Kate's noirvellas of 1940's Detective Nelle Callahan feature O.S.S. illusion flair interwoven with history's last laugh.

From early Ohio lands to Connecticut and Rhode Island shores, Kate does it right, does it big and gives it class. She's been published in *Action: Pulse Pounding Tales vol. 1 and 2*, *Bleed* (combating cancer in little kids), *February Femmes Fatales*, *Days of Madness* and others.

Encounter Kate Pilarcik, sleuth of the shadows of noir, @ her website *{at-the-bijou.blogspot.com/}*. Exchange in lively repartee at Facebook and Instagram, Twitter, GoodReads and Pinterest.

Kate absolutely thanks you for your reads...but you knew that. She promises never a dull moment.

OTHER TITLES FROM DOWN AND OUT BOOKS

See www.DownAndOutBooks.com for complete list

By J.L. Abramo
Catching Water in a Net
Clutching at Straws
Counting to Infinity
Gravesend
Chasing Charlie Chan
Circling the Runway
Brooklyn Justice

By Trey R. Barker
2,000 Miles to Open Road
Road Gig: A Novella
Exit Blood
Death is Not Forever
No Harder Prison

By Richard Barre
The Innocents
Bearing Secrets
Christmas Stories
The Ghosts of Morning
Blackheart Highway
Burning Moon
Echo Bay
Lost

By Eric Beetner (editor)
Unloaded

By Eric Beetner and JB Kohl
Over Their Heads

By Eric Beetner and
Frank Scalise
The Backlist
The Shortlist

By G.J. Brown
Falling

By Rob Brunet
Stinking Rich

By Jen Conley
Cannibals

By Tom Crowley
Vipers Tail
Murder in the Slaughterhouse

By Frank De Blase
Pine Box for a Pin-Up
Busted Valentines
and Other Dark Delights
A Cougar's Kiss

By Les Edgerton
The Genuine, Imitation,
Plastic Kidnapping

By Jack Getze
Big Numbers
Big Money
Big Mojo
Big Shoes

By Richard Godwin
Wrong Crowd
Buffalo and Sour Mash (*)

By Greg Herren (editor)
Blood on the Bayou:
Bouchercon Anthology 2016

(*)—Coming Soon

OTHER TITLES FROM DOWN AND OUT BOOKS

See www.DownAndOutBooks.com for complete list

By Jeffery Hess
Beachhead

By Matt Hilton
No Going Back
Rules of Honor
The Lawless Kind
The Devil's Anvil
No Safe Place (*)

By Jerry Kennealy
Screen Test

By Ross Klavan, Tim O'Mara
And Charles Salzberg
Triple Shot

By S.W. Lauden
Crosswise

By Andrew McAleer and
Paul D. Marks (editors)
Coast to Coast vol. 1
Coast to Coast vol. 2

By Terrence McCauley
The Devil Dogs of Belleau Wood

By Bill Moody
Czechmate
The Man in Red Square
Solo Hand
The Death of a Tenor Man
The Sound of the Trumpet
Bird Lives!

By Gary Phillips
The Perpetrators
Scoundrels (Editor)
Treacherous
3 the Hard Way

By Tom Pitts
Hustle

By Robert J. Randisi
Upon My Soul
Souls of the Dead
Envy the Dead (*)

By Ryan Sayles
The Subtle Art of Brutality
Warpath

By John Shepphird
The Shill
Kill the Shill
Beware the Shill

By Ian Thurman
Grand Trunk and Shearer

James R. Tuck (editor)
Mama Tried vol. 1
Mama Tried vol. 2 (*)

By Lono Waiwaiole
Wiley's Lament
Wiley's Shuffle
Wiley's Refrain
Dark Paradise
Leon's Legacy (*)

(*)—Coming Soon

Made in the USA
Middletown, DE
28 September 2016